HAZE

The Love Life of an Insomniac

by Jon Marcus

CHAPTER 1

THE TROUBLE WITH INSOMNIA

Late at night, most people are sleeping. However, many others are up and active, doing their nocturnal thing. Some of those things are their passions like writing or painting. Some people drink and let loose. Some are watching movies or playing video games. Some are doing their jobs.

It's 12:05 am in Manhattan. Most of the cars on the streets are cabs and rideshares. One of the taxis is driving two people in the back seat, Joel and Nancy. Joel is sleeping. Nancy is a beautiful blonde woman he just met at a party. She is watching the city scenes go by as the taxi takes them to their destination.

The cab passes one restaurant whose business is going strong. The restaurant next door though, is closed and night crews are cleaning up. At a subway stop close by, someone is walking down the stairs where a few other people are waiting on the platform for their trains. At an apartment building, paramedics are giving CPR to someone. On the next block, two homeless people are trying to sleep on the street; they have a dog companion. Elsewhere, a woman (Maja) is painting in her apartment. At a hotel a few blocks away, someone with a travel suitcase is checking in. The cab passes a police car slowly patrolling the streets. A block later, they pass a night electric crew working under the street from a manhole. The taxi is almost at Nancy's building.

Nancy: "I'm so glad we met at Gina's birthday party. I'm wide awake. Would you like to come up?"

Joel snorts in his sleep.

Cab driver: I guess not.

Joel is 6'2", in decent shape (used to run daily before insomnia set in), a good looking guy.

Nancy: Joel?

Driver: Is he ok?

Nancy: Well, he's breathing so I guess he's ok.

Driver: He must have drank a lot.

Nancy: No, not at all. Not even water.

Driver: Drugs?

Nancy: No, look at him.

Driver: The guy sleeping in the cab?

Nancy: I mean, he's not the type.

Driver: Hey, you never know. Some of the biggest doped up assholes that get in my cab dress like respectable professionals.

Nancy: I know what you mean, but this guy is not a drug user.

They arrive at Nancy's apartment.

Driver: This is your stop.

Nancy: Should I wake him?

Driver: I wish you would. I don't want to have to do that.

Nancy: Joel honey? (She nudges his shoulder).

Joel: (mumbles) Huh? What?

Nancy: Are you ok?

Joel: Oh…yeah. I have insomnia, so sometimes I nod off here and there.

Nancy: Oh. We are at my place. Would you like to come up?

Hearing this invitation, Joel immediately wakes up. Any guy would be thrilled if a woman who looked like Nancy invited him up to her apartment.

Joel: Yeah!

Joel pays and they get out of the car. The driver heads off into the night. Joel and Nancy go into her building, go up one flight and enter her apartment. She has a small dog that is watching them. As soon as she closes the door, she kisses Joel and they start making out. Then:

Nancy: Kiss my neck.

Joel: OK.

Joel enthusiastically starts kissing her neck. She breathes heavily and then the dog barks.

Nancy: Later Princess.

The dog starts scratching the door. She ignores it and takes her top off. She's wearing a purple laced bra and she has a super hot body. She takes Joel's hands and puts them on her breasts. Then she points at her cleavage and says:

Nancy: Now kiss me here.

Just then, before Joel can even move, the dog starts barking incessantly. They both stop and look at the dog.

Nancy: Oh, she really has to go. Um, do you mind?
Joel: Uh, yeah sure. Go ahead.

Joel reluctantly backs off but can't seem to let go of her breasts. He pauses as the dog keeps barking, and then removes his hands.

Nancy: I'll be back in a minute. Make yourself comfortable.

She puts her top back on. The dog is prancing.

Nancy: C'mon Princess.

She puts a leash on the dog and exits. Joel sits down on the couch. Nancy comes back seconds later.

Nancy: I forgot the waste bags. Now don't fall asleep on me.

He smiles, she leaves, and 30 seconds later he drifts off asleep. A few minutes later, Nancy returns.

Nancy: That was an unexpected mess.

She has bit of poop on her hands. Nancy sees Joel sleeping. She goes to the kitchen sink and washes her hands thoroughly while her face shows she is getting more noticeably upset with every second. Then she dries off her hands, goes to the couch and wakes Joel up.

Nancy: Wake up dude.

Joel: Huh?

Nancy: Go home and go to sleep.

Joel: What's wrong?

Nancy: You fell asleep on the ride home, I got dog poop on my hands, and then you fell asleep on my couch. I'm really not feeling great about tonight.

Joel: Oh. What if we just sleep and then maybe in the morning...

Nancy: Not a chance. Go home.

Joel unhappily says, "OK" and he leaves.

He walks to the main street, puts his hand up but no taxis come by. He doesn't have ridehsare apps. So he starts walking. He has a long walk to go to his part of town. He eventually gets to his street which is in the west side of Greenwich Village. It has lots of trees and is quiet and charming. It's narrow too. Only one apartment on the street has its lights on. That apartment is across the street from his.

Joel: Probably another insomniac.

He goes into his building, tiredly trudges up the stairs and enters his apartment. He has a big window that opens to the fire escape and overlooks the street. He looks out of it and sees the light again from the apartment across the street. He goes into his bedroom, gets undressed and gets in bed. As he pulls the covers up, he notes the time of 1:26 am. He is thinking of the beautiful woman he just blew it with. His thoughts are interspersed with his view of the clock when he sees it at 1:37, 2:03 and 2:26. He keeps tossing and turning but can't fall asleep. At 2:51, he turns on the radio. He still can't sleep. Eventually, he looks over and the clock says it's 3:17am.

Joel: Sure. Now I stay awake.

CHAPTER 2

AFTERMATH OF INSOMNIA

It's a beautiful day out. Joel is a little tired and walking around New York when his phone rings. It's his friend Gina, whose birthday party he attended last night. He answers the phone.

Joel: Hey Gina!

Gina: Hi Joel.

Joel: Your party was fun.

Gina: Thanks.

Joel: What's up?

Gina: Well, I got a call from Nancy this morning.

Joel pauses and knows he is about to be chastised. The girl club is about to invoke it's fury over something that he did with one of it's members.

Joel: Here we go.

Gina: Let me tell you about Nancy.

Joel: Uh huh.

Gina: She's smart and super hot.

Joel: I noticed both.

Gina: And she never goes home with anyone. She hasn't been with a guy in a long time. A girl who looks like that.

Joel: What a surprise.

Gina: No, listen. She gets offers, a lot of them, but she turns them all down. And she liked you. Talk about a missed opportunity.

Joel: You don't have to remind me. I couldn't help it. She seems a bit angry anyway.

Gina: She was angry cause she never gets laid, she never meets anyone she really likes and then she's primed and you fell asleep on her. Twice!

Joel: Well, she didn't have to kick me out.

Gina: What, so you could fall asleep on her a third time?

Joel: OK, she was right to kick me out.

Gina: She has trust issues. She's had a couple of bad boyfriends…this call is not about her. I called to tell you that your insomnia has been going on a long time and as a friend, I'm telling you to get help.

Joel: You seem angry.

Gina: It's not anger. It's frustration.

Unfortunately, Joel knows Gina is right. He has tried a few things and his insomnia persists. He doesn't know what to do.

CHAPTER 3

HEIGH-HO, HEIGH-HO

It's late at night. Joel is unsuccessfully trying to sleep.
He hears a clock ticking. He hears people outside
talking loudly and he gets up and wanders over to the
window. He sees them going around the corner. The
light in the apartment across the street is on.
Everything else is dark and quiet. He is tired and
groggy. He goes to bed but he can't sleep and just
lays there. He fluffs the pillow and the blanket. He still
can't get to sleep. He hears more drunk people
outside yelling as they go home.

"Hey Frank!"
"Hey Jennifer"
"Good night!"

"Good night!"

"Woo hoo!"

Its 3am. He goes to the couch and notices the light across the way is still on. He turns on the tv with the volume really soft and tries to sleep. Eventually he drifts off for three hours. He wakes up and sees the kitchen clock which reads 6am.

Joel: Time to go to work.

He gets up.

He almost falls asleep in the shower.

He is looking sleepy as he gets dressed.

He checks the fridge but there is hardly anything there. Just a pizza box and some condiments. He eats some leftover pizza, puts on his shoes which he has at the door with a bunch of other shoes, and then he goes to work.

As he makes his journey to work, he is looking and feeling tired. Other people are looking happy and peppy. People on the crowded subway notice him half asleep.

When he gets off the subway, he stops into a pharmacy. He picks up a 2-liter bottle of warm Diet Coke and a box of Lucky Charms. He walks to the check out line.

Cashier: Starting your day off with a bang?
Joel: Breakfast of champions.

He pays and goes across the street to the hospital where he works in the purchasing and supply department. He wanders into his office, goes to his cube and a co-worker comes over. It's Anjelica. She is very nice and very conscientious of others. It's comforting talking to her. She has almost a mom quality to her, although she doesn't have children. She is married and Joel thinks she will make a great mother some day.

Anjelica: Good morning sunshine.
Joel: (yawns) Good morning.
Anjelica: Whats in the bag?
Joel: Caffeine and sugar.

He removes the Diet Coke and the cereal box.

Anjelica: Lucky Charms?

Joel: They are lucky and the charms are loaded with sugar. And they're magically delicious.

Anjelica: OK. And Diet Coke for breakfast?

Joel: I've never liked coffee.

Joel opens the box of Lucky Charms and reaches in.

Anjelica: Do you need a bowl to pour that concoction into?

Joel: Lucky Charms in a bowl of Diet Coke? I'm not an animal.

He pulls out a fist full of cereal and eats the handful dry.

Joel: I love the dry marshmallows.

Then he chugs the Diet Coke from the bottle.

Anjelica: This hurts to watch.

Another co-worker, Simon, comes over. Simon is a decent guy but is a bit superficial and immature. He is in his mid 20s so it's not surprising.

Simon: That's quite a breakfast. You know, while it may wake you up, I suspect in the middle of the night it will be blasting out of you.
Joel: That's ok, I will be awake then anyway.

Their boss, Will, comes by.

Will: Meeting in 10 minutes.

Will notices the cereal and soda on Joel's desk.

Will: I assume you will get there by bouncing off the walls.

Joel quickly consumes all the Lucky Charms and Diet Coke that he can and then heads to the conference room. Everyone else is there waiting for him. They discuss a few work things and then Will brings up one last subject.

Will: Now that we've gone through all that, I think we should discuss why Joel can't sleep.

They all express their approval of this subject. Tan starts. He is also in his mid 20s but not as superficial as Simon.

Tan: How much sleep do you get per night?
Joel: I think I average about 3 hours, and that's just from pure exhaustion.
Anjelica: Joel, do you have anything causing you stress in your life?
Joel: Yeah. Insomnia.
Simon: Have you tried sleeping with classical music on?
Joel: Tried it. I liked it so much I payed attention and couldn't sleep.
Isabella: How about the TV?
Joel: Tried it too.
Anjelica: You know what works for me? Scented candles.
Joel: Not a chance. You can't get that smell out of the apartment. Besides, some of those candles have been found to have lead in the wicks and who knows

what the chemicals are in the scented wax that you breathe in for hours.

Anjelica: Huh. Maybe I should stop using them.

Tan: How about adjusting your diet? Salt and sugar affect sleep.

Joel: I ate well when I got insomnia. Now I don't eat well. Nothing has changed.

Will: Exercise is good for your general health and it affects sleep.

Joel: I'm too tired to exercise.

Isabella: Sex?

Isabella is a gorgeous woman. She has big brown eyes, long brown hair and a stunning body. They all turn and look at her.

Joel: I'm too tired to have sex.

Tan: Have you tried acupuncture?

Joel: Three times. The first time I got sleep. The second not so much. The third not at all.

Isabella: How about sleep apnea?

Everyone in the room agrees that's a good idea.

Anjelica: My husband has sleep apnea.

Simon: Have you seen a doctor?

Tan: Yeah, you should see a doctor.

Joel: Are there doctors that specialize in sleep?

Anjelica: Yes. The sleep doctor that my husband saw is on the 4th floor. Let me find his number (she looks in her phone).

Later that day, it's about 5pm. Joel is staring at the wall and watching the floaters in his eyes go back and forth when he moves his eyes. The sound of the air ventilation and co-workers typing at their computers is quite loud in his head. Then he hears people closing their computers.

Simon: Well, done for the day.

Isabella: So long.

Simon leaves. Then Tan leaves. Tan is a little introverted and often doesn't express pleasantries, use people's names in conversation or look them in the eye when talking to them. He finds looking at them distracts from his train of thought, so he looks down. Often, when he's talking to a woman, and looking down, the woman assumes he's looking at her body. It's because of that, he doesn't have a girlfriend. On the phone he's great. In person they think he's a pervert. He's noticed some make motions to cover themselves up when talking to them. He realized later why, but it doesn't occur to him while talking to them.

After he leaves, Anjelica comes over to Joel in his cube.

Anjelica: Good night Joel. Be well.
Joel: Thanks. (Anjelica leaves).

Isabella comes over and puts her hand on Joel's shoulder.

Isabella: Try to get some sleep Joel.
Joel: Thanks Isabella.

She leaves and Joel stares at the wall for a few minutes more before he snaps out of it, packs up and goes.

CHAPTER 4

DAY OFF

When he's close to home, Joel stops in a small
grocery store near his place. It's a good size for a
neighborhood grocery store; it has fresh veggies and
some good food in it. He goes there often. Today
though, Joel isn't interested in healthy food. He picks
up a few things like sugary cereal and Diet Coke. He
looked it up once and found Diet Coke has more
caffeine than other diet sodas. Then he gets in line.
Maja is the person in front of him in line. She is a local
artist. He saw her once but he's never spoken to her.
Today, they don't notice each other. Maja gets to the
front, checks out and leaves. After her, Joel does the
same. While walking home, he steps in dog poop and
doesn't notice it.

He gets home. He has a number of pairs of shoes at the door. His policy is "Shoes off at the door" because the streets of New York, or any city, have lots of disgusting stuff on them. Joel takes off his shoes by having each toe snag the heel. He puts the grocery bag on the counter, opens the fridge, takes out the pizza box and eats the last slice of pizza. Then he sits on the couch, watches TV and falls asleep on the couch. At 11:30 pm he wakes up. He stands up, stumbles into the bedroom and gets in bed. He lies there for awhile but he can't sleep. His insomnia is not just a sleeping problem; it's frustrating and annoying. In fact sometimes it's so annoying that it his annoyance keeps him from sleeping.

Eventually, he gets up and wanders into the living room. Joel has a few night lights in the electric outlets so it's never pitch black when he's tired and so he doesn't trip over furniture or doesn't have to flip lights on when walking around at night. It also makes him feel good remembering how his parents put night lights in his room when he was a little kid.

He sits on the couch and turns on a TV show. He curls up on the couch but it doesn't help him sleep. He goes to his big living room window and looks out at the city. He sees a light on in the apartment across from his. Then he sees someone on the street walking a dog. He sniffs and smells the dog poop he stepped in earlier. He thinks *what's that unpleasant smell?*

He sits on the couch staring at nothing. In a haze, while half asleep, his fingers tap buttons on his phone which opens up an app. While he isn't asleep or awake, his hand and fingers move a little and this taps things which automatically orders food from three restaurants including a few sandwiches, some sushi and a couple pizzas. Shortly after he does fall asleep.

Eventually the pizza delivery guy shows up and knocks. Joel is sleeping. The pizza guy hears snoring through the door. He knocks louder and still hears snoring. Then he leaves the pizzas at the foot of the door.

The next food delivery guy knocks and Joel wakes up. The guy waits but Joels doesn't know why he woke up and just lies there on the couch. The delivery guy puts the food next to the pizza boxes and leaves. Joel sees the clock which reads 2:45am. He thinks *"Did someone knock at the door?"* He goes to the door, looks through the peep hole, sees nothing and then goes back to the couch and tries to go back to sleep. He can't. He stares at the ceiling.

At 6am Joels gives up and gets ready for work. He is groggy during his morning routine. As he opens the door and leaves, he steps on the food boxes. He pauses in confusion. Then he looks at his phone and yells:

Joel: Damnit, I did it again.

He takes the food in.

Joel: First things first, I'm deleting this app. I can walk to get my own food anyway. (He deletes the app). Eight hour old warm sushi, could be lethal. (He throws it out). But the pizza is ok, even if I did step on the box.

He is putting it in the fridge when he notices the brown substance on the box. He smells it and exclaims:

Joel: What the fuck!

He looks at the shoes that he is wearing and sees brown along the edges of one of them. He takes it off and smells it.

Joel: Dog shit. I hope its from a dog. Damn it, I hate this city.

He takes out a hefty bag from under the sink. And starts to throw his shoes and the food in it. Then he realizes he stepped in the dog poop on his floor while only wearing socks. Plus he tracked it around. That was the bad smell he noticed last night.

Joel: Damn It! It's everywhere.

He takes his socks off and sits on the kitchen counter while cleaning his feet. Then he carefully steps on the floor calculating where he wouldn't have stepped. He gets cleaning supplies from under the sing and then gets on his hands and knees and starts scrubbing and throwing things out.

Joel: At least I don't have carpeting.

45 minutes later, when he thinks the apartment is cleaned, he decides he needs a break from everything.

Joel: Fuck this. I'm going to take the day off. What can I do today?

He calls his boss and says he is taking a sick day. It's early so his boss isn't in and Joel can just leave the message without a discussion as to why. He thinks he is done cleaning but he still smells the dog poop. He doesn't know why. It could just be residual in the air or it could be from the garbage bag containing all the contaminated things he just cleaned with or it could be that he still has some on his feet plus now his knees.

He smells the couch but fortunately there isn't any on the couch. Taking his shoes off at the door all the time saved him from soiling the couch. Then he checks the bed and its safe too. Then he sits on the bed and tries pulling his feet up to his nose but he can't contort that much. So he goes to the kitchen, gets paper towel and then sits on the couch, wipes his feet and knees and smells the paper towel. Bingo. His feet still have poop on them.

He gets a steel wool from under the kitchen sink, wets it and scrubs his feet and knees. Then he puts alcohol on the paper towel and wipes his feet with that. Then he gets a scrunge, sprays bleach on it and wipes his feet and knees with that. Then he wets a bunch of paper towels again and pours baking soda on them and wipes his feet and knees. Then he uses alcohol again. Lastly, he tries soap and water. He lathers up his knees and wipes with paper towels. Then he does the same for each foot.

He thinks he must be clean but realizes he forgot to check the kitchen floor before he sat up on the counter. So when he steps on the floor. He could get that on his feet again. His thought now is wondering if there is something he could step on. There are a few dish drying towels there. He leans over to get them, and then tries his best to get them to drop flat on the floor. They don't land perfect but they are pretty close. He gently lowers himself onto the towels and then gets on his knees to smell the floor. It still smells like poop.

He has to start all over again, first cleaning the floor. But he is low on cleaning supplies and almost out of paper towels. So he has to go to the store for more. He realizes with poop on his feet, he will basically be ruining a pair of shoes. Which should he ruin? The ones he stepped in the poop with were already in the garbage bag. He picks a pair of old sneakers. After putting them on, he makes sure his hands are clean. They are

Joel: Whew!

He puts on some rubber gloves and takes the bag of all the stuff out with him. He ties it up and throws it in the garbage in the basement. Then he goes to the store and buys LOTS of cleaning supplies and paper towels.

Cashier: Looks like a fun day

Joel: Yeah. Fun.

Two hours later, after he re-scrubbed the floor, dried it, made sure his hands, feet and knees were clean, plus took a shower, Joel decides to go to a baseball game. He checks the schedules and finds the Yankees are playing a day game today. He hops on the subway uptown. Then he transfers to another subway to get to Yankee Stadium in the Bronx.

He buys a ticket at the ticket booth, eats a hotdog and waits for the game to start. By the 4th inning, he is fast asleep. The fans deposit their empty cups and other garbage on him. One put a hot dog bun on his head. Some are throwing popcorn at him. In the 6th inning, the TV cameras spot him.

Broadcaster: Well, he looks like he's enjoying the game.

Later, while Joel is still sleeping, a foul ball just misses his head.

Fan 1: Damn, he's out.
Fan 2: I wonder if he's drunk.
Fan 3: or on drugs.
Fan 1: He doesn't have a beer cup. Maybe he took something before the game.

Joel sleeps through the whole game. After it ends and the fans are leaving, the ones that walk past him look at him wondering what the story behind him is. Most assume he passed out drunk. Afterwards, an usher wakes him up.

Usher: Hey man. Get up.
Joel: Huh? What?
Usher: The game's over.

Joel looks around to see the stadium almost empty.

Joel: Oh, geeze. I missed the whole game?

Usher: Yeah. We were watching you. Listen, you seem like a good guy. Have you ever heard of alcoholics anonymous?

Joel is embarrassed. He gets up, leaves the stadium and takes the subways back to to Manhattan. The one he gets on goes to the east side. Joel lives on the west side. So he takes the cross town bus. The bus is full and a few people are standing. Almost everyone is tapping on their phones. He finds the only open seat which is a window seat next to a big guy, shabbily dressed. The guy doesn't look homeless so he doesn't know why no one is sitting there. He squeezes past the big guy and sits down.

Bus Rider: Excuse me sir. You are on my side.
Joel: Huh?
Bus Rider: You are on my side. Move over!

The guy is getting upset.

Joel: (says calmly) What do you mean, on your side?
Bus Rider: You see this seat in front of us? It has a dividing line in the middle between the two seats and

your leg is over on my side. Now move it back to your side.

Joel pulls his leg towards him. He is uncomfortably scrunched in the area.

Joel: Is that better?

He gets no answer. He looks out the window and relaxes. As he does, his leg relaxes and drifts over the mid point.

Bus Rider: Hey! How many times do I have to tell you? Driver! Driver! This man is on my side. Stop the bus and make him move.
Joel: Tell you what, I'll just stand the rest of the way.

Joel stands up, moves to the isle and grabs a handrail. The person next to him has a smile and is looking at Joel.

Bus Passenger: A few minutes before you got on, I was sitting there.

As he's walking home from the bus stop, he comes across a woman, Maja, painting a street scene. It's the same woman who was in front of him in line at the grocery store recently. He looks at the painting and at the view that she sees in front of her and back at the painting.

Joel: I like it.
Maja: Thanks!

Joel smiles at her and takes a second as she is very attractive. She has a beautiful face, wears no makeup and she dresses down, for comfort. They smile at each other. Then Joel leaves and goes home.

CHAPTER 5

THE DOCTOR

It's 1am and Joel can't sleep. He hears sounds in the building like floors creaking, a toilet flushing and a loud neighbor laughing while watching the TV. He also hears a clock ticking. He thinks, *"I don't own a clock that ticks. My kitchen clock has dials, but it's silent. Why do I hear a clock ticking? Maybe I'm losing my mind."*

Except for those occasional building sounds, it's very quiet. He gets up, goes into the living room and sits on the couch. Then he hears a car horn beeping. He also notices a spider web in a corner of the ceiling. He gets off the couch, pulls a chair over to that corner of the apartment and stands on the chair to closely look at the spider. It doesn't make a move. Then he gets down off the chair, goes back to the couch and stares at nothing. He can't sleep; he just sits and stares. Eventually around 3am, his head starts bobbing as he starts to drift off to sleep. However, the head bobbing wakes him up. He curls up on the couch and sleeps until 5am. Then he lies awake on the couch, eyes open, for an hour trying to get back to sleep. At 6am he gives up.

Joel: Well, I guess I got a total of four hours of sleep. That's a record. Maybe I should have walked around the city instead of falling asleep at the Yankee game.

He gets up.

Joel is groggy in the shower. He gets dressed, eats a bowl of Frosted Flakes and drinks some Diet Coke. The news is on TV.

News: Get ready folks. A heat wave is on the way. Mid 90s expected for the next 10 days.
Joel: Sure, who can't sleep in a hot apartment.

He drinks the excess milk in the bowl, puts the bowl in the sink, adds water and goes to work.

Mid morning, Joel goes to the appointment that he set up with the sleep doctor. The waiting room has advertisements for a few things including one for a CPAP machine and one for a pillow. The pillow ad has a sample pillow next to it. Joel thinks it's cruel to put a pillow in a sleep doctor's waiting room. It's like they are taunting you. Then the nurse comes out and takes Joel back to the exam room. He sits down on the exam table and looks at the medical posters in that room. He also sees an autographed photo from a player on the other New York baseball team, the Mets. After a few minutes, the doctor comes in.

Doctor: Hi Joel. Nice to meet you.
Joel: You too.
Doctor: OK, you are having sleeping problems. How long has this been going on?
Joel: About a year and a half.
Doctor: How much sleep do you get each night?
Joel: I think about 3 hours per night. Sometimes not even that. Most nights I spend in a haze half asleep. It

feels like I have enough energy so I can't drift off. But I'm groggy all day. Yesterday I fell asleep at a baseball game.

Doctor: Little league?

Joel: Yankees

Doctor: Yeah, little league. (Joel smiles) Have any overnight guests mentioned snoring?

Joel: Minimal.

Doctor: You look thin, so I guess no weight gain since the sleep issues arose.

Joel: None

Doctor: Do you go to bed the same time every night?

Joel: Bed? Yes. Sleep? No.

Doctor: Have you tried sleeping pills?

Joel: No, I'm not a fan of popping pills.

Doctor: Have you tried anything else?

Joel: A few things. Nothing works. Some people suggested I get tested for sleep apnea. What do you think?

Doctor: I'm guessing that's not the problem here, but you never know. Let me see your throat. Open up.

The doctor looks in Joel's throat with a lighted instrument.

Doctor: Your tonsils and uvula are small. So thats good.

Joel: They could be a problem?

Doctor: Oh yeah. I've had patients that the whole cause of their sleep apnea were huge tonsils and uvula. They obstructed good airflow. We cut them out and the problem went away.

Joel: Whats a uvula?

Doctor: That thing that hangs down in the back of your throat.

Joel: I never considered that would be cut out. OK. What exactly is sleep apnea?

Doctor: It's when you don't get good airflow during sleep. Something in those peoples' throats causes it.

Joel: What do you mean, something?

Doctor: It could be the tonsils or soft tissue further down the back of the throat. Some people when they sleep, for some reason their throat relaxes so much that it gently collapses on itself. So then air can't get through.

Joel: Huh.

Doctor: And without air, there is no oxygen. So when the body uses up enough oxygen in the blood, it sends an urgent signal to the brain that wakes them up. This happens all night so they aren't getting deep sleep, if much sleep at all.

Joel: Huh.

Doctor: Plus the low oxygen levels can eventually damage parts of the body including the heart and cause all sorts of health problems.

Joel: Oh.

Doctor: We can run tests while you sleep and see if thats the cause. How does your schedule look to spend a night in a sleep lab?

Joel: So, you think I should get the sleep test?

Doctor: We can set it up.

Joel sets up the sleep lab appointment with a scheduler. Then he goes back to work. Part of his job is that once per week, he talks to salespeople at a window where they come by. Today is that day. He looks tired and bored. He opens up the window and there are a number of salespeople waiting.

Salesperson 1: Good morning

Joel: Hi. Watcha got?

Salesperson 1: These gloves are a higher quality than the brand you are using. The ones for lab workers are even slightly higher quality than that. Plus they are 50 cents cheaper per box.

Joel: I can take your information but I seriously doubt they will change. The established contracts are long term.

The sales people all have their pitches. The next one comes to the window.

Salesperson 2: We sell cleaning supplies that are rated the highest quality.

Joel takes his product info and the next approaches. Then the next. Then the next. And the next....

Salesperson 3: Syringes of various volumes.
Salesperson 4: Grade A oxygen masks.
Salesperson 5: The best liquid hand soap.
Salesperson 6: High quality test tubes.
Salesperson 7: Linens and pillows for gurneys.
Salesperson 8: Very comfortable crutches and canes of various materials.

Salesperson 9: Cups, plates and eating utensils.

Salesperson 10: It's the highest quality commercial toilet paper money can buy.

At the end of the day, people at work are packing up. Joel seems awake.

Isabella: Are you heading out Joel or are you going to sleep here?

Joel: I'm catching up on work. I fell behind being groggy.

Isabella: Good night.

Joel: Night.

He works till 7:30. As soon as he walks out the front door of the hospital, the heat wave hits him. Everyone outside looks overheated.

Joel: Oh yeah. Heat wave. I'm sure my apartment is a comfortable 95 degrees inside. I wonder if you can die falling asleep in a sauna.

CHAPTER 6

THE HEAT WAVE

Joel goes home on the subway. Everyone in the subway looks overheated. He thinks: "*I thought these things had air conditioning. The fans are on. Are they piping in the heat from outside?*" He gets off the train and walks up the stairs to street level. It's almost sunset. He goes to the corner grocery. As he's about to enter, he sees Maja, the artist, painting across the street again. He enters the market while thinking about her and how beautiful she was when she looked at him before. The memory of her eyes stirs emotion in him. For now through, he has to buy something.

Joel: "I've been eating too much sugar. I need vegetables."

Meanwhile, across the street, Maja's cell phone rings.

Maja: Hi mom. Yeah, everything is good? How are you? Good. And how's Paris? Really? Oh, that's great. Yes. I'm painting at the moment. A street scene. We have a heat wave starting today. It's really hot. Yeah, I'm on a crowded corner too. On that note, can I call you back some other time? OK. OK. Bye.

Joel buys a large pre-made chef's salad and a six pack of bottled water. He leaves and sees Maja is still there. He crosses the street to get to her.

Joel: Ah, my local artist friend.
Maja: Oh hi!
Joel: Here, it's hot. I just bought a bunch of water. Have one.
Maja: Oh, great! (She drinks) Thank you so much.
Joel: Let me see your painting. (He looks at her painting).
Maja: What do you think?

Joel: Wow, it's really good.

Maja: You are too kind.

Joel: No, I really like it. I love those New York apartment buildings with the huge staircases. (He points at it). I'm Joel.

Maja: Maja.

Joel: Maja. Is that with a Y or a J?

Maja: J! Not many people know to ask.

Joel: I assume you live around here.

Maja: Yes I do.

Joel: Cool. What's the next thing you are going to paint?

Maja: Not sure.

Joel: Well, the heat wave just started. What about painting sweaty tired people?

She laughs. Joel likes the sound of her laugh.

Maja: Maybe.

Joel: OK, see you around.

Maja: Yeah.

Joel heads back across the street and Maja watches him for a couple seconds. When he gets home, his apartment is really hot. He opens the window and turns on a fan. He puts on shorts, takes the salad out of the bag and goes out on the fire escape to eat. He hears jazz coming from someone's apartment. It fills the air. He doesn't know which apartment it's coming from but the music is the perfect volume and style to set the mood on a hot summer evening on a cozy New York block. As he's looking around, he sees Maja come from around the corner with her stuff and go into the building across the street. He is happily surprised.

A few minutes later, the window across the street that always has the light on late at night, opens up and Maja crawls onto the fire escape. She flaps her shirt to cool herself off. She drinks from the water bottle that Joel gave her and then pours the rest of the water over her. It falls on some of the pedestrians below and they look upset and try to see where it came from. Maja yells down to them.

Maja: Sorry!

Joel laughs. She looks across the street and sees Joel. He smiles and waves and she points at him enthusiastically.

Maja: Is that salad?
Joel: Yup.
Maja: I'll be right back.

She goes into her place and comes back with her own salad. She crawls out onto her fire escape and starts to eat. Maja and Joels are eating their salads together across the street on fire escapes in the heat.

They each look at the other a couple times as they eat.

Maja: This street looks nice at sunset.

Joel's mouth is full and he tries to say something but he can't speak. He makes a motion of agreement. Maja laughs. Joel chews, swallows and then asks her:

Joel: How long have you lived there?
Maja: Uhhhh seven years. You?

Joel: About a year and a half.

Maja: Did you grow up in the city?

Joel: Seattle.

Maja: Oh. I heard it's nice there.

Joel: It is. I like it here too. Where are you from?

Maja: New York. Well, here and New Jersey. My parents got divorced when I was in high school. I went back and forth a lot.

Joel: Mine are divorced too.

They see a neighbor barbecuing on his fire escape.

Joel: I could never do that.

Maja: Not your style?

Joel: I like the idea. But I'd probably knock over the grill. Someone would get burned.

Maja: Someone or the building would go up in flames.

Joel: Right. How long have you been painting?

Maja: Since I moved in here.

Joel: You like the Village?

Maja: Yeah. I needed inspiration and a picturesque neighborhood.

Joel: Cool. On that note, the subway station wasn't even slightly cool today. You would think being underground and shaded from the Sun would make it cool.

Maja: I just read about that. The heat is from a few things.

Joel: Let's hear it.

Maja: The ground above the platforms radiates heat onto the platforms,

Joel: OK.

Maja: Plus the heat on the street pushes into cooler areas like on the platforms because of an energy difference.

Joel: Really.

Maja: And then the air conditioners in the trains expel heat.

Joel: The air conditioners?

Maja: Yeah. I guess air conditioners work not only by throwing cool air into a room but they also have a second system that absorbs heat and throws it outside the room. So for the subway trains, the hot air would get thrown into the tunnels or...

Joel: ...the platforms

Maja: Right.

Joel: The blowing air on my train was hot today.

Maja: Well, the A/C was probably broken.

She changes the subject.

Maja: What do you do for work?
Joel: Purchasing and supply for a hospital.
Maja: Nice.
Joel: It's OK. I like it.
The **neighbor thats barbecuing** on his fire escape
yells to his wife, "Honey, can you bring me the
barbecue sauce?"

Maja and Joel are both noticing the beautiful sunset.

Maja: I love this street. I like watching the cars slowly
navigate through it. I like to imagine how it was before
cars. Charming horse drawn carriages and much
quieter.
Joel: That sounds nice but a friend of mine is a
historian and he was telling me the city was quite
filthy back then. Horses pulled carriages but they
pulled everything in those carriages: food carts,
garbage collection carts, taxi carts, furniture moving
carts, mail carts, funeral carts. Those horse powered
carts hauled anything and everything in the city.

Maja: I don't see the problem.

Joel: There were horses everywhere.

Maja: Yeah, so?

Joel: With horses there is manure and with a lot of horses everywhere, there was a lot of manure everywhere. Everywhere. The sewer system wasn't good either.

Maja: OK. Shot my dream all to hell.

Joel: You know those iconic New York brownstones with those big elevated staircases like I saw in your painting today?

Maja: Yeah.

Joel: Those big staircases were developed just so people could avoid all the manure on the streets. It piled up. It was a huge health problem. And then when it rained...

Maja: Enough!

A couple from another apartment building go out on their fire escape and cuddle.

Maja: All this yelling across the street is starting to hurt my voice.

Joel: Like to take a walk?

Maja: Well…the streets look manure free, so OK.

Joel likes how smart and witty Maja is. They go into their respective apartments and then meet downstairs.

Maja: Let's go this way. There are some art galleries. I would like to see what you think of the art.
Joel: OK.

CHAPTER 7

NIGHT WALK

Maja: The only thing missing on a hot summer night in New York are fireflies.

Joel: I've never seen them.

Maja: Oh, they are great. I remember in the summer, New Jersey had lots of fireflies. I love them.

Maja and Joel are walking and talking in the warm summer night. Joel is thinking how he likes that he doesn't feel like he has to put on airs or make a great facade with Maja. Maja senses Joel is being himself. It makes her feel comfortable and she likes that she doesn't feel she has to decipher who he really is. Then they come upon a number of art galleries.

Maja: OK, this is a photographer I know. (They walk up to the art gallery window). What do you think?

Joel: Uh...is this done by a friend of yours?

Maja: Just be honest.

Joel: Honest huh. I won't offend you?

Maja: No. Lets hear it. Although I get the feeling I already know.

Joel: Not my thing.

Maja: Why?

Joel contemplates whether he should tell her the truth.

Maja: C'mon

Joel: It's horrible and ridiculous.

Maja: This is called fine art.

Joel: I've heard the phrase. I think they call it that because if they didn't, nobody would buy it.

Maja smiles.

Joel continues: Calling it fine art is like putting lipstick on a pig. It's why news anchors have to wear suits. Because no one would respect the bubble gum versions of the news they spew out if they didn't dress up.

Maja: Don't hold back. Give it to me straight.

Joel smiles at her. They go to the next gallery.

Maja: How about this?
Joel: This is nice.
Maja: Yeah. I like it too.

They look at the art for a moment. Then they go to the next gallery. Maja looks at Joel and waits to hear his analysis. The art is dark and ominous. It has lots of black, gray and red. Plus it has spikes, chains and things that look like a torture chamber.

Maja: I think I know.
Joel: You do know. Do people actually buy this?
Maja: Yes.
Joel: People who own a dungeon, right? (Maja laughs.) Or the ever growing market of dominatrixes; just to get their clients in the mood.
Maja: Well, I know this artist and, don't tell anyone but, yes, he has a few of those women's numbers

saved in his phone.

Joel laughs. They look at a few more galleries. Then they go to the last one.

Maja: What do you think?
Joel: Well, it's OK, Nothing special. It looks like something I would see in an office building.

Maja laughs.

Maja: That's what she specializes in.
Joel: Wait. Except that one.

Joel points to a painting of to the side and in the back.

Maja: Oh?
Joel: This is different. I like it. (pause) Huh.
Maja: What.
Joel: It looks like the style I saw when you were painting on the street. Is this yours?
Maja: You have a good eye. And good taste.

Maja puts her hand on his shoulder.

Joel: It is yours?

Maja: Yes.

Joel: I do have good taste.

Maja smiles. They walk home quietly and along the way she takes his arm. Then they get to her building.

Maja: This was nice.

Joel: Yeah.

There is a pause as the romantic tension builds. They both move in and share a nice kiss and a hug.

Maja: I'll see you soon.

She goes into her building. Joel walks across the street to his and then says to himself, "I don't have her number."

He goes inside. When he gets to his apartment, he puts a fan near the window and turns it on. He sees Maja's light on. He smiles. It's 10pm. Joel gets into bed thinking of Maja and the night they just shared.

He still can't sleep but he is happy. At 3am, he isn't happy; he's just tired.

Joel: Damnit.

He goes into the living room and looks outside. Maja's light is off. His apartment has cooled down. He turns off the fan and sits on the couch. At 4am he falls asleep. At 5:30am he wakes up.

CHAPTER 8

THE SLEEP LAB

It's noon the next day. Joel is tired, of course. His co-workers are discussing where to go for lunch.

Simon: I could go for a burger.

Tan: In this heat?

Isabella: Tan is right. Let's go to that sandwich and salad place across the street.

Simon: You go ahead. I know an Irish pub close by that is air conditioned and makes great soda bread. Plus, I can watch a soccer game there.

Isabella: Air conditioned?

Anjelica: Yeah, let's go there.

They all agree. They start to leave.

Tan: Joel, want to join us for lunch?

Joel: Thanks no. I'm going to try to take a nap.

They leave and Joel sleeps in his chair. The co-workers are enjoying lunch together. The pub is busy. Many people are watching the soccer game, including Simon. His co-workers talk like he is not there, because he's concentrating on the soccer game. At one point Simon sees a woman at the bar sitting alone. She looks over at him, he smiles, she looks back at the TV and is clearly not interested in him. Then he starts talking to his co-workers.

Back at the office, Joel is sitting in his chair, sleeping soundly. He eventually he falls off his chair, narrowly missing hitting his head on the desk. He wakes up as he's falling. He sees that he is on the ground and decides to remain on the floor and sleep. When the co-workers return, they find Joel on the floor.

Simon: Oh my god, he's dead.

Isabella: Joel!

Isabella rushes to Joel, gets on her knees and reacting to what Simon said, thinks about taking Joel's pulse, she instead shakes him a little on the shoulder.

Isabella: Joel. Are you ok?
Joel: Huh. Oh. Yeah.

Anjelica and Tan gasp in relief.

Isabella: What happened?
Joel: I was sitting in my chair and then I fell asleep and then I just fell.

He gets up.

Joel: I'm fine.

Isabella looks shaken. She is looking deeply at Joel. He looks her in the eyes and there is a second or two when everyone just pauses in the moment.

Joel: I'm fine. Really.

Isabella gets up, clams down and composes herself. Then she looks at Simon.

Isabella: He's dead?
Simon: What?
Isabella: Drama queen.

She walks off to her cube.

Late in the afternoon, Joel goes home a bit early to eat and gets his stuff for the sleep study. The subway is hot and crowded. He is groggy. He packs an overnight bag with clothes. At 7pm he leaves and takes the subway back to the hospital. It's not as crowded but it's still as hot thanks to the heat wave. He finds the sleep lab and walks in.

They give him some papers to sign and then the sleep technician walks Joel into the back where the lab is which has a bed in it and lots of medical equipment.

Sleep Tech 1: OK Joel. Change into something to sleep in and then we will get you prepped for the sleep study.

They leave and close the door. Joel changes into a t-shirt and gym shorts. Then he goes out the door and tells them he is ready. Two people come in and wheel over a cart with many electrical cords on it and some electrical boxes they plug the cords into. They also bring over a chair.

Sleep tech 1: Please have a seat.
Joel: OK. (He sits down) How does this work?
Sleep Tech 2: We attach a bunch of wires to you and then you go to sleep and we measure to see how deep your sleep is and how your oxygen levels and pulse are.
Sleep Tech 1: And if it's sleep apnea, we wake you up and put a CPAP mask on you.
Joel: What's CPAP.
Sleep Tech 1: It stands for Continuous Positive Air Pressure.
Joel: Huh?

Sleep Tech 1: It's a machine that sends slightly pressurized room air into your throat that will keep it open while you sleep.

Sleep Tech 2: It sends the air from the CPAP machine, here (she points to the CPAP machine), through a hose, then through a mask that we put on your face.

Joel: And people can sleep all wired up like this and with a mask and hose stuck to their face?

Sleep Tech 2: Yup.

Joel: OK. Lets go.

Sleep Tech 2: OK. First we will put the electrodes on you.

Joel: Alright.

He looks at the wires.

Joel: Thats a lot of electrodes.

Sleep Tech 1: Yep.

They start attaching the electrodes to various places on his scalp and other parts of his body like his chest and legs.

Joel: And people can really sleep with all this on them too?

Sleep Tech 2: You'd be surprised what people can sleep through.

Eventually they are done. He is covered in electrodes and cords.

Sleep Tech 1: Do you need to go to the bathroom before you go to sleep?

Joel: (laughs) Now you ask me?

He carefully walks into the bathroom to pee. The electrodes are all attached through a central box and the box is held on a rod like an IV bag would be held. He wheels it in with him and when he's done, wheels it all out with him.

Sleep Tech 1: OK, hop into bed and we'll be in the next room. We have a camera, a microphone and a speaker in here if you need to talk to us.

Joel: OK.

Joel gets in bed and they hook the other ends of the electrode cords into various machines. Then they leave and Joels tries to go to sleep. Amazingly he drifts off to sleep quickly. One hour later:

Sleep Tech 1: This guy doesn't have sleep apnea.
Sleep Tech 2: Not even close. Let's let him sleep through the night.
Sleep tech 1: This guy in the other room has got it bad though. I will go in and hook him up to the CPAP.

At 6am, Joel wakes up. He slept the whole night through and he feels rested. Knowing the microphone is in there, he says out loud:

Joel: I'm awake.

One of the technicians comes in.

Sleep tech 2: Sleep well?
Joel: Yes, great thanks.
Sleep tech 2: Good. Let me disconnect all these wires.

Joel: I assume you found something since I slept well for the first time in a long time.

Sleep tech 2: We'll give the data to the doctor and you can discuss it with them.

That morning, Joel is at his office early because he slept in the hospital. He's wide awake and full of energy because for the first time in ages. One by one, the others eventually come in.

Joel: Hey Anjelica.

Anjelica: Yes?

Joel: I saw your sleep doctor and spent last night in the sleep lab.

Anjelica: Really! How did it go?

Joel: I don't know what they did but I slept like a baby.

Anjelica: Oh that's fantastic!

Joel: Yeah, thanks. I have a follow up with the doctor today to discuss what they found.

Anjelica: Great! Tell me what he says.

Later that day, in the doctor's office…

Doctor: You don't have sleep apnea.

Joel: What?

Doctor: All the data shows perfect sleep. EEGs and everything. They didn't even put a mask on you it was so good.

Joel: No mask?

Joel thinks about last night and remembers they never did wake him up and put the CPAP mask on him.

Joel: Oh, right. How come I slept so well there?

Doctor: I don't know. I'm guessing your sleep issues are psychological. Have you talked to a shrink?

Back at Joel's office, Joel walks in from after the doctor's appointment and goes to Anjelica's cube.

Joel: He said I don't have sleep apnea.

Anjelica: What? I don't understand.

Joel: Neither do I.

Anjelica: But you said you slept well there?

Joel: I did.

Anjelica: Was that after they put the CPAP mask on you?

Joel: They never put it on me. They wired me up and I slept all night. I assumed they did something to help me sleep, but they didn't.

Anjelica: So what's causing your sleep problem?

Joel: I don't know.

Anjelica: Maybe you should talk to a shrink?

CHAPTER 9

TAKE A CRUISE

After work, Joel is wondering whats causing his sleep problem as he's walking in to his neighborhood grocery store. Maja is walking out with just a water.

Joel: Maja!

Maja: Hi Joel. Going to get another salad?

Joel: I don't know what I want. I'm glad I ran into you. I don't have your phone number.

Maja: Oh right. I realized that later that night. Give me your phone.

He unlocks his phone and she types her number in.

Joel: Cool. (He texts her). There, you have mine too. (Maja smiles).

Maja: This heat is brutal.

Joel: Yes it is. You know, I bet it's cooler over the water. Want to see if we can catch a night cruise?

Maja: Ooo. Let's go.

Joel and Maja head over to 5th Avenue. There is lots of traffic.

Maja: South Street Seaport?

Joel: Yeah.

The Friday rush hour is extremely busy and slow.

Maja: OK, how?

Joel: You know, I never downloaded any ride-share apps on my phone.

Maja: Thats OK. I take cabs. Cabs are fully insured and the drivers are managed.

Joel: Well, we won't get a cab on a Friday at rush hour. (They see a double decker tour bus stopped close by). Let's try this. (They run to the bus). Hi, do you stop at South Street Seaport?

Tour Bus Driver: That's our next stop. Got a ticket?

Joel: No. How much are they.

Tour Bus Driver: Oh, well you have to get 'em online or from the main office.

Joel: What if we give you ten bucks.

Tour Bus Driver: We can't take locals unless they buy a ticket. Sorry.

Joel: How about 40.

Tour Bus Driver: Uhhh.

Joel: 50?

The driver put out his hand discreetly. Joel gives him the money. Maja likes this. The driver makes a head motion to get on. Joel motions to Maja to go first. She smiles and gets on the bus. Joel follows. The bus is three quarters full but they find a seat easily.

Tour Bus Driver: OK, folks. Next stop, South Street Seaport.

It's nearing sunset. The bus slowly meanders it's way through the bustling streets at rush hour, over to the South Street Seaport where the cruise boats are docked. If it wasn't for the traffic, it would be a really nice ride surrounded by all the activity. When they get there, Joel and Maja hop off the bus, run over to the ticket window and get their tickets.

Joel: Got 2 tickets left?
Ticket Booth Seller: Yes we do.
Joel: Great. I'll take 'em.

Joel pays for the tickets while Maja looks around at the area. She loves the city.

Ticket Booth Seller: Hurry up, they are about to pull away.

Joel and Maja run onto the boat and look for a place by the rail to stand. The boat crew closes the gate and un-ropes the boat from the dock. As the boat pulls away from the dock, Maja takes Joel's hand.

Maja: It must be 10 degrees cooler here at the shore.
Joel: Yeah.
Boat Announcer: Welcome aboard everyone. It's a great night for a cruise. As we pull away, you can see the Brooklyn Bridge behind us. It opened in 1883 and

it was at that time the longest suspension bridge anywhere. The towers are made of granite, limestone and cement.

On the right, you can see the Freedom Tower. It was built of course to memorialize the Twin Towers. At 1,776 feet tall, the number is not a coincidence, it is the tallest building in the Western hemisphere.

This is a great sunset to see the Statue of Liberty.

The Statue of Liberty was a gift to the United States from France in 1886. It was shipped here in 350 pieces and assembled where it stands today. She is quite a sight.

Just north of Liberty Island is Ellis Island. Between 1892 and 1954, over 12 million immigrants came to the United States through Ellis Island. Most people don't realize this but outside of people of the Native American heritage, everyone's family in the US came here via immigration. Ellis Island is now a museum to commemorate all the people who came to America in the past. It is definitely worth a visit.

Maja: So tell me something about your life Joel.

Joel: You know, I've never been able to answer that question.

Maja: OK. Tell me something that is happening or on your mind recently.

Joel: Outside of I'm having the time of my life being with you?

Maja: (Maja smiles). Yes.

Joel: OK. Well the big thing going on with me is I have insomnia.

Maja: Really?

Joel: Yeah.

Maja: How bad?

Joel: I get a couple hours of bad sleep per night.

Maja: Do you know whats causing it?

Joel: No, and I've tried everything. Acupuncture, TV, music. I even went to a doctor recently and did a sleep study. He has no idea.

Maja: Lovely.

Joel: You know what's funny?

Maja: What?

Joel: Often when I've been up in the middle of the night, I saw your light on. I was wondering who lived there and what they did so late every night.

Maja: Oh, that is funny.

Joel: So now it's your turn. What do you do so late into the night every night?

Maja: I paint or watch a movie or something. I'm just a night person.

Joel: So no drama.

Maja: No.

Joel: No nightly parties or strange voodoo worshipping or anything.

Maja: Haha. No.

Joel: Well. Mystery solved.

Maja: I guess so.

Joel: And here we are looking at New York from a boat.

Maja takes his hand again.

Maja: Yup. You know, I used to have a sleeping problem.

Joel: Used to? How did you beat it?

Maja: I realized I am a night person. So I didn't beat it. I let nature make the decision. Now I stay up generally till early morning, like 4am-ish. The city is nice and quiet then too. I love it.

Joel: Great solution.

Maja: Yeah, it works for me.

Joel: I have a day job so I can't try that. But I've never really been a night person, so it's probably not my problem.

Maja: Well, we'll examine the options over time.

When the boat returns, Maja and Joel make their way back home. They walk holding hands to Maja's apartment. They walk through her door. There are many paintings of hers propped up on the floor and many photos of New York City on the walls. She also has a pile of shoes at the door like Joel does. So each of them takes off their shoes off in their apartments. This fact makes Joel feel like they are good for each other. Maja turns and looks at him. They start kissing and she takes his hand and leads him into her bedroom. They have passionate loving sex. Afterwards, only one word is spoken by each.

Joel: Wow.

Maja: Yeah.

They spoon and he falls asleep quickly and sleeps through the night. When he is sleeping deeply, Maja gets up, eats something and reads a book on the couch. Eventually she goes back to bed at 3am and puts her arm around him.

A few hours later, around 6am, while Maja is sleeping deeply, Joel wakes up. He puts on his underwear and walks around her place looking at all the photos and paintings. He really likes the art she makes. He also likes the photos of old New York. She is sleeping soundly and he figures he will leave and let her sleep. As he is getting dressed, Maja wakes up.

Maja: Good morning.

Joel: Good morning beautiful. (She smiles.)

Maja: You seemed to sleep ok.

Joel: I did. You must be good for me.

Maja: I'm glad.

Joel: I can stick around but you said you usually go to sleep late so...

Maja: Yeah, I didn't go to sleep until 3am. We'll talk soon.

They kiss, Joel leaves and Maja goes back to sleep.

CHAPTER 10

DINNER AND DIAGNOSIS

Inspired by Maja's art, Joel wants to take a second look at the art in the galleries where he and Maja went the other night. He heads over there himself. He walks in and looks at the various art pieces.

Loretta: May I help you?
Joel: Uh, just looking.
Loretta: OK. I'm Loretta. Feel free to look around.

Joel looks at the paintings again which reinforces his thought that they are made for office buildings. Eventually he works his way over to Maja's painting. He really does like it. Her romantic thoughts of New

York really come out in her painting. After a few minutes:

Joel: Out of curiosity.
Loretta: Yes?
Joel: Do you have anything else by this artist?
Loretta: Ah. She is wonderful. No, there were more but they already sold.
Joel: OK, thanks for your time.
Joel leaves and goes to look at the other galleries that they saw plus some others that he didn't see with Maja.

At 11:30 Joel gets on the subway uptown. He feels like going to a Yankee game. The game starts around 1pm. He changes trains again and gets on one going to the Bronx. Its packed and many of the people are wearing Yankee shorts and hats. When he gets off the subway, he goes to the ticket window to buy a ticket. They are sold out. So he goes to one of the many pubs in the area to look for a ticket. He asks the doorman at one of them and the guy says has often has tickets that he sells. He shows 5 of them to Joels who buys one from him.

He goes in to the stadium and there are lots of people walking around in the walkways. There are also lots of vendors selling food and souvenirs. He stands there and takes in the sight. An older guy (Joel guesses around 65) is standing next to him with a Yankee cap on.

Older Yankee Fan: It's nice huh?
Joel: It is.
Older Yankee Fan: When I was a kid, my first game was at the original Yankee Stadium. This area with the vendors was lIke a dark canyon. Really big, old and dark. I remember walking through it with my dad and when we went out to the seating area, the white stadium structure, the green in the field and blue seats were lit up like we were entering a different world.
Joel: I've heard that same account from an uncle of mine. It must have been something else.
Older Yankee Fan: Yeah, but this is nice. They did a good job.

They both look around for a minute taking in the sight.

Older Yankee Fan: Hey, enjoy the game.
Joel: Yeah. It was good meeting you.

The old guy walks off. Joel buys a program, walks to his seat and sits down. A hot dog vendor walks buy and he buys one. This time, he is awake after some good sleep. He has a great time even though the Yankees ended up losing.

After the game, Joel takes the subways home, heads up to street level and goes to the neighborhood grocery store. In the store, he and Maja bump into each other.

Maja: Oh how funny.
Joel: You know, I'm starting to really love this place.
Maja: What did you do today?
Joel: I went to a Yankee game.
Maja: Did they win?
Joel: No, but I had a good time AND I stayed awake for it.

Maja: Nice.

Joel: And before that I went to those galleries you brought me to. And a few others.

Maja: Oh. What did you think?

Joel: You know. Some of it I liked and some I thought was for dungeons.

Maja: Haha. Did you meet Loretta?

Joel: I did but I didn't say I knew you. I felt that might be intrusive.

Maja: Wow, you are considerate.

Joel: I guess so. Are you hungry?

Maja: A little.

Joel: How about I cook you dinner?

Maja: OK. But for me it's only lunch.

Joel: Oh, right.

Maja: What did you have in mind to make?

Joel: Ever have Shrimp Scampi?

They buy ingredients and wine then go to Joel's apartment. Joel thinks, "What is it about this girl? She is so honest that her closeness makes my head spin." He doesn't feel like he has to play games and he doesn't feel like she's judging him.

So many people go on dates hiding their true selves from each other, it's unnerving. We can all tell when this is happening and it feels dishonest so the date is kind of doomed from the start. Maybe they do this because they were dumped for stupid reasons and hurt by others in the past so they developed this way of acting to get through to initial few dates without getting dumped again. Maybe it's from a basic insecurity, like they don't think the other person will like them unless they put on a good face. But we can all sense the facade, and we all don't like it. So we tell ourselves its understandable, a sign of baggage which we all have. With Maja though, she doesn't seem to put on the facade.

They get to Joel's apartment and both take off their shoes. Joel likes that she just gets it. The fan has been running in his window the whole day because the long lasting heat wave is still going. Joel puts the grocery bags on the counter and starts to unpack everything.

Maja: What can I do?

Joel: How about, I wash and chop the herbs. You open the wine and shave some of this cheese we got. Oh, and start the water boiling for the pasta.

Maja: OK. What kind of cheese is it?

Joel: It's Parmigiano Reggiano. It's like the best Parmesan cheese out there.

Maja: Oh!

Joel: If you have an urge to chop herbs, that's ok too.

Maja: No. No. You seem to be in the zone.

Joel starts washing and chopping herbs.

Maja: So, what do you got there?

Joel: I little oregano, a little basil and a lot of garlic.

Maja: Yum! What else is in Scampi?

Joel: Just olive oil, butter, shrimp and maybe a little seasoning.

Maja: That's it?

Joel: That's it.

Maja: No onions, mushrooms, capers.

Joel: No. I like those too but they don't work with this dish. I actually love mushrooms but one time I put them in Scampi and it was awful.

Maja: OK. Red or white wine?

Joel: The only real rule with wines is white wine with seafood. Some people will tell you anything goes. But really, white with seafood.

Maja: Are you a world class chef?

Joel: Ha. No, but I worked at this really great Italian restaurant in college and I learned a few things.

Maja: I get the feeling I'm in for a treat.

Joel: I hope so. I don't know a lot of dishes, but I like this one.

Joel is cleaning the shrimp and removing the tails and shells. Maja opens the wine and pours some in two glasses. She takes a drink.

Maja: Like a sip?

Joel: Yes please.

She comes over with her glass and carefully tips it in his mouth so he doesn't have to touch it since his hands are covered with raw seafood. After drinking, Joel just smiles at her. She smiles back. She puts the water on the stove and turns it on.

Maja: Ooo, induction cooking. No gas.

Joel: Yeah.

Then Maja starts shaving the cheese. They stand there doing their prep work silently and glancing over at one another occasionally. In a few minutes they are done and ready to cook.

Joel: OK. Here's the fun part.
Maja: OK.
Joel: The cooking takes just a few minutes. The water is boiling, the flame is low and the pan is heated.
Maja: Geeze, I feel like I'm watching a cooking show.
(Joel smiles.)
Joel: So. We add the olive oil, butter and a little white wine.

He adds them.

Joel: The butter is melting, the oil is starting to simmer. Now add the garlic.

Maja adds the garlic.

Joel: In just a bit, when you smell the garlic...

Maja: I smell it.

Joel: We add the shrimp and the herbs. (Joel adds them). And now we boil the pasta.

Maja puts the pasta in the boiling water.

Joel: Angel hair pasta just takes 2 minutes to cook. The shrimp looks cooked on the sides so we flip them all over.

He flips each shrimp using tongs.

Joel: The pasta should be done now. Take a fork and test one of the strands to see if its cooked.

Maja tests the pasta and gives Joel a thumbs up.

Joel: OK. Want to strain it and add half to each plate?

She does and then he pours the cooked food over the pasta.

Maja: Oh, yum.

Joel: Would you care for some cracked pepper?

Maja: OK.

Joel cracks pepper from a pepper mill over each plate. Then he puts the two plates on the table (Seated at 90° from each other - not across the table from each other). Then they sit down.

Maja: Oh, we forgot to slice the bread.
Joel: That's OK. It's more fun to tear it.

He tears tears off a piece for himself and puts the remaining on a plate in the center of the table. Then Maja does the same.

Maja: Oh, this smells amazing. (She takes a bite.) Oh my god, this IS amazing!
Joel: Yeah, it turned out OK.
Maja: OK? It's fantastic!

She leans over and kisses him. Then she tears a piece of bread off for herself, dips it in the sauce and eats it. There is a happy atmosphere in the room between Joel and Maja. Eventually the finish eating.

Maja: Joel, anytime you want to cook for me, is OK.

Maja raises her glass, he follows suit, they clink them together and take a drink. Then Maja gets out of her chair and straddles him in his. They start making out. Soon they are taking each others' clothes off in the chair. They run over to the bed and have sex. It's very passionate. One of her legs is wrapped around his waist and the other his leg as he's on top of her. She just keeps pulling him towards her the whole time. Afterwards:

Maja: It's 9pm.
Joel: Yeah? Are you saying you want to go?
Maja: No. You have insomnia so I don't know what to do. Although you slept great at my place.
Joel: Yeah. I slept the night before too in a sleep lab when they were testing me.
Maja: Really!
Joel: Yeah, but they didn't find anything.
Maja: Hmmmmm.
Joel: Yeah. What do you think?
Maja: Maybe it's this place?
Joel: What do you mean?

Maja: I took a lot of psych classes in school. Can I ask you some questions?

Joel: Anything.

Maja: You said you've been here a year and a half.

Joel: Right.

Maja: Alone?

Joel: (He answers reluctantly) No. I moved in here with a girlfriend.

Maja: OK. Tell me about her.

Joel: Uh, Maja, you and I just had sex. We're naked in bed. Are you sure you want to go down this road?

Maja: Definitely. I have a psych degree. Give me the details.

Joel: You have a psych degree?

Maja: Actually a Masters.

Joel: What? Why…Why aren't you...

Maja: It's a long story. I'll tell you all that later. Let's talk about the ex first.

Joel: No wait. How did you go from Psych Masters to Artist?

Maja: The short version is I was taking patients in a PhD program and I realized that although I like psychology, I just couldn't do this the rest of my life.

Joel: OK. That makes sense.

Maja: Now. the girlfriend.

A thought occurs to Maja which concerns her and leads to her next question.

Maja: She is an ex, right?
Joel: Yeah.

Maja feels relieved.

Maja: Good. By the way, what's her name?
Joel: I just refer to her as Medusa.

Maja laughs.

Maja: Medusa from Greek mythology. Was her hair made of snakes?
Joel: Yes and she turned men to stone. But not in a good way.
Maja: OK, So you moved in here with her a year and a half ago. When did the insomnia start?
Joel: Actually, a month or two after we moved in.

Maja makes a circular motion with her hand in a way
to tell him to keep talking.

Joel: The insomnia ruined the relationship. I was tired
all the time and she would get upset because I
couldn't sleep well; I didn't want to go out to
restaurants or parties or anything.
Maja: So what happened?
Joel: I tried all sorts of stuff but nothing worked.
Maja: And?
Joel: She got fed up and moved out.
Maja: How was the relationship the first two months.
Joel: It was ok.
Maja: And before moving in?
Joel: It was ok.
Maja: OK? It was OK?
Joel: Yeah.
Maja: Joel, you moved in together. The relationship
should have been fucking fantastic. C'mon. Dig deep.
What was the deal?

Joel thinks about it.

Joel: You are right. We never should have moved in together. I guess I wanted to have a mature relationship and moving in together seemed mature, but she was a mistake.

Maja: OK. Now, what remains?

Joel: Nothing. I don't have any feelings for her. In fact, I'm glad she's gone.

Maja: Good, but I don't mean that. When she left, what did she take with her?

Joel: Actually, hardly anything.

Maja: So all this furniture that's here, you bought?

Joel: Well, it was my money that bought it but she was the one who picked it all out. When she left, she just packed her clothes and moved in with a friend.

Maja: What stuff that's here did she buy and what stuff did you pick out?

Joel: Geeze, you know. She picked it all out. Except the TV.

Maja: Boom! That's it!

Joel: What's it? The TV?

Maja: No. The cause of your insomnia. All this stuff reminds you of her. The insomnia didn't ruin the relationship. The insomnia came about as a byproduct of the bad relationship you were in. It was your body's defense against your shitty girlfriend. Some people deal with stress and bad emotional stuff by using booze or drugs. Some people fight or some develop weird sexual fetishes. You didn't know what to do with the stress of living with this terrible person, Medusa, and in suppressing the stress, your subconscious and body reacted with insomnia.

Joel: Huh.

Maja: Psych tip, you really can't suppress anything. You have to deal with it head on because eventually it all comes to the surface and bubbles out.

Joel: I can see that.

Maja: So now, even though she's gone, you are constantly reminded of her because of all this stuff in your apartment. All this stuff is like a bunch of ghosts. The stuff remains so the subconscious defense against the memories and the feelings that they bring up, remains. And so the insomnia remains.

Joel: Holy crap.

Maja: Bottom line, getting rid of your insomnia is easy. You have to get rid of all the stuff your ex bought.

Joel: Maja, that's everything.

Maja: I'm telling you. Get rid of it and you'll get rid of the insomnia.

Joel: No, I mean it's literally everything. I won't have dishes or a bed or towels or even a shower curtain.

Maja: So what. You can't sleep! It's wiping you out. Get rid of it.

Joel: All I'll have left is half my clothes and the TV.

Maja: Half your clothes?

Joel: She bought some.

Maja: Geeze, you were just a project to her. You are so better off without someone like that.

Joel: Definitely. How would I get rid of my stuff? It's too much to haul it all to Goodwill and a garage sale will take too long.

Maja: How about you put an ad on Craigslist. "Saturday only. I'm giving away everything in my apartment. Couch, dishes, electronics, bed, everything." I bet it will all be gone in a couple hours.

Joel: (laughs) Yeah, there will be a mob scene. Well, it's an interesting theory.

Maja: Theory? I'm right.

Joel likes her intelligence.

Joel: OK. Here's the thing. It sounds logical, but the thing with psychology is it's intangible so it's kind of conceptual so it's hard to tell if it's right or if it just sounds good.

Maja: OK, I see your point.

Joel: And more importantly, in trying out this theory, I would have nothing left and would have to sleep on the floor.

Maja: Buy a mattress.

Joel: Buy a mattress? They are expensive. I would rather buy a couch and sleep on that.

Maja: OK. Do that.

Joel looks at her as he is thinking about the logistics of sex and sleeping on a couch. Maja instinctively knows what he's thinking. She replies.

Maja: Yeah yeah. Sex on the couch every time is kind of pathetic.

Joel loves that she can tune into him like that. Maja is smart plus she gets him.

Joel: Well, I'll definitely think about it.

Maja curls up to him and pulls his arm around her. She looks at the clock and the time lapses a few hours into midnight.

Maja: You aren't asleep, are you?

Joel: No. But I'm thoroughly enjoying this.

Maja: Why don't we go across the street to my place and we can sleep there.

Joel: Test your theory out?

Maja: That too.

Joel: OK.

They get dressed and leave. Only their underwear is in the bedroom; half of their clothes are in the kitchen. He loves watching her put her bra and panties on. When they are fully dressed, they walk across the street and go into Maja's place.

As they are undressing to get in bed, they are both filled with desire again. They start taking their clothes of faster like it's a race. Then they jump under the sheets.

Maja: Oh wait.

Joel: Huh?

Maja goes into the other room, grabs her purse, takes out a condom, open the wrapper and rolls the condom onto Joel. No foreplay this time. Maja immediately grabs him and slides him into her. Then they fuck wildly.

Afterwards, she gets off of him and goes into the bathroom to clean up. When she returns she gets under the sheets and spoons him. He pretty quickly falls asleep. When she hears him sleeping, she says:

Maja: Theory nothing. I am so right.

The next day, Maja wakes up at noon. Joel is gone. She goes into the kitchen and a note is on the counter. We hear Joel's voice saying the words as Maja reads it.

Joel's voice: *Hiya Maja. I slept well. Maybe your theory is right.*

Maja: Of course it is.

Joel's voice: *I don't want to crowd you and blow it, so I will give you a day or two or three. But you can crowd me whenever you want. I will try to remember to lock the door on the way out.*

Maja goes to the door and checks. He did lock it. She smiles.

CHAPTER 11

GINA AND SEAN

Joel is in his apartment. He is well rested after sleeping at Maja's and he is feeling happy. On the other hand, he is concerned that he will mess up the relationship somehow. Why? Because he always does. Usually its because in his enthusiasm, he over-contacts the woman. Not knowing what to do, he calls his friend, Gina, to see what she thinks from a woman's frame of reference.

Joel: Hi Gina.

Gina: Hey there. What's up?

Joel: I need a woman's advice.

Gina: Let's hear it. Oh, but first, Nancy asked about you. I can't believe it but I think you may still have a shot with her.

Joel: Nancy? Oh, right. Purple bra.

Gina: Huh?

Joel: Nothing.

Suddenly, with the vision of Nancy taking off her shirt in his mind, Joel forgot what he was going to say.

Joel: Uh, Nancy. That's OK. No. I met someone. Someone great.

Gina: Really?! Do tell.

Joel: Well, it's funny. Every night that I can't sleep...

Gina: ...You mean every night.

Joel: Yeah. I see someone's light in an apartment across the street. When the heat wave started, I was on the fire escape eating something and the woman in that apartment came out and we started talking to each other across the street.

Gina: You met each other on fire escapes?

Joel: Well, I had said hello to her a few times bumping into her in the neighborhood. But we never really had a conversation until we were on the fire escapes in the heat.

Gina: I love it.

Joel: She's really great.

Gina: OK. So what do you need advice for?

Joel: Well, no matter how much any woman seems to like me, she always finds a reason to tell me doing something wrong. And then she breaks up with me. So I want to talk this out.

Gina: OK. By the way, what's her name?

Joel: Maja.

Gina: OK. Go on.

Joel: Maybe I am crowding all these women but this one, I keep running into her and we keep spending huge amounts of time together.

Gina: Wow.

Joel: Yeah.

Gina: You like her. Don't crowd this one.

Joel: I know. But this one feels different. I don't feel like I have to walk on eggshells with her.

Gina: It's early?

Joel: Yeah.

Gina: Give her space.

Joel: You don't understand.

Gina: Joel.

Joel: We've already spent two nights together and get this. When I'm at her place, I can sleep.

Gina: Whoa!

Joel: Yeah.

Gina: Still. Learn from your track record. Women want space.

Joel: Can you explain to me what the space thing is all about? How come women complain that guys just treat them like meat but when you like one and want to get to know her, they want you to back off?

Gina: Because so many men do crowd them and so many men come on strong and it makes them feel like a piece of meat. Like they are put in a position where the guy wants to get her to do what <u>he</u> wants. So when any guy comes around, they emotionally back off to assess and see how he acts because they are leery because of all the bad experiences before you. It's not you. It's prior experience with all the jerks which are 95% of the guys out there.

Joel: So I'm being punished because of all the idiots that approached her before me.

Gina's husband, Sean, enters.

Gina: Punished isn't the right word, but yeah.

Sean: Who's being punished?

Gina: Joel

Sean: Hi Joel.

Joel: Hi Sean.

Sean: Who's punishing him.

Gina: Women.

Sean laughs.

Sean: You can't win man. Gina, put him on speaker phone. (She does).

Gina: I was just telling him women want space.

Sean: Bullshit. Women want to be pursued.

Gina: That too.

Joel: They want space and they want to be pursued. Women don't know what they want.

Gina: We want it all.

Sean: Yeah, they contradict. You can't win.

Joel: I've asked out women and they don't exactly respond so I have to ask them again.

Sean: See? They want the chase.

Joel: But it's rude of them to pretend not to notice and make you ask again. Not to mention it's kind of humiliating for the guy.

Sean: And if you pursue them the wrong way, they will punish you.

Joel: Well what's the right way?

Sean: Who knows buddy.

Joel: And after you ask them out again, inside you are saying to yourself, "Fuck this."

Gina: Mmm hmm.

Joel: I've had women get upset because I tried to kiss them at the end of a date and then I've had women get upset that I didn't make a move.

Joel is getting upset. He stands up and starts pacing in his apartment.

Joel: Then I've had women who I had an amazing first date with, which ended with hours of sex and then they wont even return my calls. I mean, women rip on men for doing this but they do the same thing.

Gina: Maybe you weren't that good in bed.

Joel: Who, me?

He thinks about it.

Joel: Naaaaaaa…
Sean: They just want power and control man.
Gina: Excuse me?
Sean: Its true.

Gina is not amused and gives Sean the evil eye.

Gina: Please my darling. Explain your theory.
Sean: Don't take it personally man. I know women who only like guys who treat them like garbage and I know women who only chase money and then there are the ones who want to control everything. And none of them will tell you what they want because it reveals their secret plans to try to control everyone and everything. Also, what they want changes every 3 minutes.

Gina is still giving Sean the evil eye.

Sean: Except Gina; she's the greatest.
Gina: Good save. Yeah Joel. It sucks being on your end of all this.

Sean: Yup.

Joel: And they wont even tell me why. It's like I'm playing a guessing game with a 5 year old. Do you know how fricking annoying and gut wrenching it is that they won't just tell you and they expect that I'm clairvoyant.

Joel's pacing is getting faster and he is getting more animated while on the call.

Sean: Yup.

Gina: I've heard these stories before from lots of guys. I'm sorry you go through this.

Joel: As for calling them, all women don't have the same timetable to feel when they want to be called. I mean, one might want a week and another might want a day. And if I wait a week, they might meet someone else...which has happened. How do we know when to call them?

Gina: You seem angry.

Joel: It's not anger. It's frustration.

Gina: All I can say is if they meet someone else, then all you can do is say it just wasn't meant to be. Maybe that guy really turned them on or maybe the woman is playing the field, in which case you can't win anyway and you are wasting your time.

Sean: Or maybe they found a guy with lots of money and trust me, even if you are rich, you really don't want a woman who chases money.

Joel: Yeah, it's basically prostitution.

Gina: Yup. Hey baby, did you get the Mercedes detailed?

Sean: Yeah.

Gina: They always think they can fall in love with anyone so they chase the money, but it doesn't work like that and they end up wasting their lives working the money, and waste the guy's life pretending to like him. Whatever the case, all you can do is move on.

Joel: There!

Gina: What.

Joel: All I can do is move on. The women look for perfect guys, which don't exist, so then they make the guys move on and so the guys can't understand why these women who they thought they did have a connection with, tell them to hit the road.

Joel is raising his voice now. While still pacing.

Joel: And so after this happens a few times, they just start playing the odds and playing the field to beat the odds.

Sean: Yup

Joel: And then the women sense the guys are playing the field so <u>they</u> move on. And it's a never ending circle that both sides created. And they both lie to get through it and eventually no one trusts anyone and it's a mess.

Gina: Yup. Admit it Joel; women AND men are all fucking crazy. We live our lives in an insane asylum.

Sean: No argument here.

Gina: So, what are you going to do with Maja? (Joel's phone beeps.)

Joel: Oh. I just got a text from Maja It says, "Got your note. I'm going to an artist retreat for a few days. Painting in the woods with other women. Call you when I get back."

Gina: OK. So your decision was made by the universe.

Joel: Right, but she communicated. That's all I ask.

Joel is now calm and sits down.

Joel: And now I don't have to play the guessing game.

Gina: She sounds cool.

Joel: Yes, she, is.

Gina: Do this. Text her back a smiley face and <u>only</u> a smiley face.

Joel texts back a smiley face.

Joel: Done.

Gina: Good boy.

Joel laughs.

Joel: Thanks Gina.

Gina: You're welcome.

Joel: You too Sean.

Sean: Any time buddy.

CHAPTER 12

MAJA'S IN THE WOODS AND JOEL CAN'T SLEEP

Maja is at the artist retreat with other women and painting nature scenes outdoors. It's a great place to paint and also to get away from the city.

They are tucked away on a hillside. Birds are chirping. There are lots of trees, some of which are fruit bearing which attract deer who come by and eat the fruit. A small waterfall is close by. At sunset, Maja just looks at the nature around her and relaxes.

Later that night, back in New York, Joel can't sleep. By 2:30am, he's in a groggy haze again. He is utterly exhausted but not sleepy. He can't even nod off for an hour. His head has been on the pillow but half the time his eyes are wide open. He's contemplating life and human existence as he stares at things in the room. He sees a spider crawling out of the tissues box next to his bed. It rests on top of the tissues. Then another comes out. Then a few more. Then centipedes and ticks and other bugs emerge from the tissues box. Some of the bugs start flying and some land on the bed and make their way to the pillow. A flying roach lands on Joel's cheek as a spider crawls in his ear. Then Joel gasps and snaps out of it. Nothing is there; it was all his imagination in his insane drowsiness. He sits up.

Joel: This sucks.

He goes into the the living room. He looks across the street and Maja's lights are off. He turns on the TV and sits on the couch. It's now 3:30am and he still can't sleep.

Joel: Maybe Maja is right and I should get rid of all this stuff.

He tries to sleep on the couch. He drifts off around 4:30 am and at 6am the alarm goes off.

Joel enters his office first thing in the morning. He is the only one there. Eventually Isabella gets to work before the others and walks over to Joel. She looks stunning.

Isabella: You look exhausted.
Joel: Then it matches how I feel.
Isabella: Let me know if I can help.

She touches his shoulder as she walks off and goes to her cube. Joel wonders if she is interested in him.

Later that morning, Anjelica is working the sales window. Joel hears all the sales people pitching their products to her.

Salesperson 11: These are the best catheters anywhere. They can slide right into any orifice.

Later that night, Joel can't sleep again. It's 1:45am. He goes into the living room and looks across the street. Maja's lights are off. He lies down on the couch. He looks around the room and starts hallucinating that ghosts are coming out of all the things his ex bought.

Joel: Why did Maja have to use a ghost analogy. (He watches them floating). Misery acquaints a man with strange bedfellows. Maybe the ghosts can sing me a lullaby?

They don't. They just stare at him. He blinks his eyes and they are gone.

Joel: Fair weather friends.

The next day, Maja is painting at the retreat when her cell phone rings.

Maja: Hi mom. I'm at an artist retreat. Yeah, it's nice to get away from the city and breathe fresh air.

Maja's Mother: Take a cell phone picture and send it to me.

Maja: OK.

Maja's Mother: How long will you be there?

Maja: I'll be going back to the city tomorrow.

Maja's Mother: Any news to report?

Maja: Well, I'm seeing someone.

Maja's Mother: Oh?

Maja: He's a great guy. His name is Joel and he lives across the street from me.

Maja's Mother: You met him without a dating app. Good for you.

Maja: Tell me about it.

Maja's Mother: Well, I'll leave you to your fun.

Maja: OK. I'll talk to you soon.

They hang up. Maja takes a cell phone pic and sends it.

Camille: Why didn't you tell her?

Maja's Mother: She's on a retreat. Besides there's nothing to tell. I'll wait until I get the results of the biopsy.

At 3am, Joel can't sleep. He gets up from bed and walks over to the couch. On the way, he looks across the street and Maja's lights are off. He lies down on the couch and the ghosts come out of the furniture again.

Joel: Well don't just stare at me. Say something.

They just float in position looking at him.

Joel: C'mon.

They don't respond.

Joel: Out of curiosity, do you all know each other?

There is no answer.

Joel: Did you grow up together or did you meet in my place?

No response. The ghosts are just floating and staring.

Joel: Do you know my ex? Medusa? Did she tell you to haunt my place?

The ghosts still don't respond. Just more floating and staring.

Joel: Hey, what's it like being a ghost?
        If all you do is float, I would think it sucks.

The ghosts just float and stare at him. Joel hears drunk people outside.

Drunk 1: Yea!
Drunk 2: Yea!

They've upset a neighbor.

Neighbor: Shut up assholes!
Drunk 1: Hey fuck you man!
Drunk 2: Yeah fuck you!

The two drunks laugh.

Drunk 1: We're gonna stay here all night!

Drunk 2: I love New York!

The neighbor gets up, fills a bucket of water. Goes to the open window and dumps the water on the drunks.

Drunk 1: Hey fuck you!
Neighbor: Next time it will be alcohol followed up with lit matches.

The drunks leave.

Joel: I love New York.

He looks around the room and there are a lot of ghosts in it. A lot. He roles over so his back is to the ghosts. Then he drifts off to sleep.

The next morning, just before sunrise, Joel wakes up after a few hours sleep to a room full of ghosts staring at him.

Joel: You're all still here? Good morning.

They don't respond.

Joel: Rude ghosts. Get out of here!

He waves his hands like he's trying to clear smoke form the room. They all disappear. He starts his morning routine.

He steps out of the shower, he puts on a towel and cautiously goes into the main room to see if the ghosts are there. They aren't. He then cautiously goes into his bedroom to see if the ghosts are there. They aren't. He gets dressed and goes to work. At this time of the morning, there aren't as many people commuting yet. It's nice.

Joel is at his desk at work before the others.

Anjelica: Good morning. (Joel mumbles). Still not sleeping I see.

Tan enters. Then Isabella comes in the door.

Anjelica: Trying anything new?

Joel: No, but someone gave me a theory I'm considering.

Tan: What's that?

Joel: Well, I've started seeing this woman. And every time I stay at her place, I can sleep.

Isabella tries to hide her disappointment.

Joel: And we talked it out and the insomnia started when I was living with my ex. So she thinks it's caused by being surrounded with all the stuff my ex brought into the place.

Anjelica: Oh.

Joel: And she suggested I get rid of it all.

Tan: What do you think?

Joel: I'm considering it. But if it doesn't work, I'll be sitting in an empty apartment still not sleeping.

Isabella leaves to go to her cube. She sits down and looks sad.

CHAPTER 13

OUT OF THE WOODS

After work, Joel goes into the store.

Joel: I always seem to get a second wind when I'm going home.

He picks up a few things. And checks out.

Cashier: Think this heat will ever end?
Joel: They said in a couple days. It's nice and cool in here though.
Cashier: Yup, thank god. Paper or plastic?
Joel: Unless it's raining, paper. (The cashier packs the bag while Joel pays for it). Thanks.

Joel walks in his building's front door. As he's walking up the steps, a car stops across the street. Maja gets out and goes in her building. Joel enters his place and starts unpacking his groceries. His phone rings. The caller ID says Maja.

Joel: Hi!

Maja: Hi. I just got back.

Joel: I just got home from work.

Maja: Like some company?

Joel: Absolutely.

Maja can't wait to see Joel. She goes across the street and when Joel opens the door, she jumps on him and kisses him. Before they know it, they are on the floor half naked.

Maja: This hardwood floor is not comfortable.

Joel: Yeah, my knees hurt. Bed?

Maja: Yup.

They run over to the bed and have sex half clothed. Afterwards, they look deeply in each others' eyes.

Maja: Hi.

Joel: Hi. This week without you was hell. (She kisses him).

Maja: Did you sleep at all?

Joel: Nope. On that note, thanks for putting the idea in my mind that the furniture here has ghosts. I've been seeing them all week. (Maja laughs.)

Maja: Anything happen?

Joel: Yeah. At one point I tried to have a conversation with them but they don't do anything but float there. You know. Maybe instead of selling everything, I should bring in an exorcist.

Maja: Oh, I would love to see that.

Joel: Yeah?

Maja: Make sure I'm here so I can watch.

Joel: OK.

Maja: Hey, are you hungry?

Joel: What are you in the mood for?

Maja: Diner food.

They get dressed and discuss options for diners they know of. They decide on a place and walk hand in hand in the night to it.

Joel: There is nothing like a New York diner.

Maja: Agreed. New Jersey has some good ones too.

Joel: Yes. Sometimes, if I can't sleep, I will go to a diner at 3am just to be around people and not go crazy in the silence of my apartment.

Maja: It's really too bad the ghosts don't talk.

Joel: (Joel laughs). Yeah right. I can't believe I'm awake. Once I fell asleep in a noisy crowded bar. Someone caught me as I was about to fall off the stool. The owner kicked me out; they thought I was drunk.

Maja: Awwwww.

Joel: I also fell asleep at a rock concert, at a Yankee game, at a Broadway show and at work of course.

Maja: Well, when we are done here, how about we go back to my place and you can sleep there. It's ghost free.

Joel: Sounds like a good plan.

They arrive at the diner, find a booth with a table juke box and sit down. Maja is fishing through the music selection at the table's jukebox.

Maja: Geese, look at this selection. Van Halen, Mozart, Nina Simone…

Diner Waitress: Hi. Do you folks know what you'd like?

Joel motions to let Maja go first. She picks up her menu.

Maja: Is the Beef Stroganoff any good?

Diner Waitress: The cook is Russian and the recipe is his mom's.

Maja: I'll get that.

Joel: Open face turkey sandwich, stuffing and mashed potatoes.

Waitress: Anything to drink?

Joel and Maja both say "water." The waitress leaves.

Joel: Do they have anything from the Blues Brothers?

Maja: Oh, I love that movie. (She flips through the songs) Yes! Aretha Franklin. Think.

Joel puts the money in the jukebox, Maja presses the buttons and the song starts playing along with the video on the TVs in the diner. People in the diner start singing along or air playing instruments. The waitresses groove while serving food and the cooks shake it while cooking. Some patrons dance. In the video, the saxophone player is walking on the counter while playing. No one in the diner is doing that though. Everyone in the diner loves the song. When it ends, everything goes back to normal.

Joel: I wonder what would happen if we played the Van Halen song in there.

The speakers start playing Mozart and they just enjoy that. Eventually their food comes out. Maja loves the beef stroganoff and Joel loves his diner Turney dinner.

After dinner, they walk back to Maja's apartment and just go to sleep. Joel is spooning Maja. In a little bit, Maja gets up and watches a movie on her computer. At one point she washes dishes and accidentally drops a pan in the sink. It makes a lot of noise. Joel doesn't wake up. He sleeps through everything. At 3am, Maja goes back to bed.

CHAPTER 14

MAJA LEAVES

It's the weekend and Joel's is taking a walk. He is in the East Village on St. Mark's Place. He stops and stares at the building across the street. He doesn't know why but it creates a feeling of déjà vu. Then a homeless person sitting on the ground in back of him, talks to him.

Homeless Person: Something ring a bell?
Joel: Yeah. There is something about this building. But I don't know what it is. I feel I know it for some reason.
Homeless Person: I know what it is.

Joel turns around to see he has been talking to a homeless person.

Joel: Oh? Are you psychic?

Homeless Person: You do recognize it. It's a known building.

Joel: Known?

Homeless Person: Famous. But you don't know why.

Joel: Right.

Homeless Person: I'll tell you for a dollar.

Joel wonders what the homeless person knows and why he doesn't. He looks at the building again but can't figure it out. He reaches into his pocket, opens his wallet and takes out money.

Joel: Here you go.

Homeless Person: Thanks. Do you know the band Led Zeppelin?

Joel: Of course.

Homeless Person: Thats the building on the cover of their album Physical Graffiti.

Joel turns and look at it.

Joel: Oh yeah. They are from England so I assumed that building was in England.

He takes out his wallet again and removes another bill.

Joel: Here's another 5. Thanks.
Homeless Person: Thank you.

Joel wanders off. A few minutes later, his phone rings. The caller ID says it's Gina.

Joel: Hi Gina.
Gina: Hey, just wanted to check in. Did you call Maja?
Joel: You will be proud to know I didn't, but when she got back she called me.
Gina: Wow, I'm impressed.
Joel: With her or with me?
Gina: Both. You two seem good for each other.
Joel: Yeah. And and for the first time in a week, I slept last night.
Gina: She's your insomnia cure.
Joel: Maybe.
Gina: What are you up to today?

Joel: I'm off to buy her flowers.

Gina: Lovely.

They hang up and Joel walks into a florist shop.

Joel: Hi. I would like to buy a dozen red roses.

Florist: You got it. Oh actually, we are out.

Joel: Huh.

Florist: How about we make a bouquet of other nice flowers? Everyone gets roses anyway.

Joel: OK.

Florist: Would you like a vase?

Joel: No. Just wrap them up and I will take them.

The florist makes a nice arrangement. Joel pays for it and leaves. He walks over to Maja's place with the flowers. He knocks on the door. Maja opens.

Joel: Flower delivery for you ma'am. (Maja hugs him.)

Maja: They are beautiful. Come in. Let me find something to put them in.

Joel: I just realized, you don't own a TV.

Maja: Yeah, I just watch what I want on my phone or computer.

Maja's phone is on the kitchen counter where Joel is standing. He's watching her look around for a vase when the phone starts vibrating.

Joel: Hey, your phone's vibrating and the caller ID says it's your mom.
Maja: Thanks. Feel like saying hello to my mom?
Joel: OK.

Maja wants him to talk to her mother. Joel feels he is about to cross a line. A good line. He answers the call.

Joel: This is Maja's phone. Can I help you.
Maja's Mother: Hi, is Maja there?
Joel: Yeah, she asked me to answer the phone. Just a minute.
Maja's Mother: Is this Joel?
Joel: Yes it is.

It makes Joel feel good that Maja has evidently told her mom about him.

Maja's Mother: Hi Joel. I'm Maja's mother. It's nice to meet you.

Joel: You too. Where are you calling from?

Maja's Mother: France.

Joel: Wow. Oh, here's Maja.

Maja: Hi mom.

Maja's Mother: He seems nice.

Maja: He is nice. And he just bought me flowers. Anything important or can we talk later?

Maja's Mother: Actually, there is something important.

Joel is watching Maja. Maja is just listening and Joels watches her face gets very serious. She gasps.

Maja: What do the doctors say? When is the surgery? Ok, I'm going to fly out there. No mom. No. I'm heading out there. I will buy a ticket and get there as soon as possible. OK.

She hangs up.

Maja: My mom was diagnosed with cancer.

Joel: Oh no. What kind?

Maja: Ovarian.

Joel: How is she?

Maja: She is getting surgery in a few days. They are going to take out the whole reproductive system. Ovaries, uterus, everything.

Joel: Oh Geeze.

Maja: I have to pack. I'm going to fly out to her in Paris.

Joel: Ok. Let me know if I can help.

Maja: Thanks.

She kisses him, walks him to the door, gives him a big hug. He leaves. She goes to her computer and looks for a ticket. First available flight. One leaves in 30 minutes. It could take an hour to get to the airport, never mind go through international checks before getting on the plane. That doesn't even include packing. There is one that leaves in 4 hours. She books it and hurries into her bedroom to pack.

Maja leaves and goes to the closest main street to hail a taxi. She is there for 10 minutes as cabs with passengers drive by. Finally one pulls up. She throws her bags in the back seat and gets in.

Maja: JFK Airport please. International departures.

When they reach the airport, she pays the driver, grabs her bags and runs in the terminal to the ticket counter.

Maja: Hi, I have a reservation.

CHAPTER 15

BREAK

Late at night, Joel can't sleep again. He is lying on his couch awake. The ghosts are there staring at him.

Joel: If you aren't going to talk, the least you could do is make ghost sounds or haunted house noises. You know. Ooooooooo.....

<u>Texting</u>

Joel's phone makes a sound. It's a text from Maja. "Thinking of you. Loved the flowers."
Joel responds. "Thinking of you too. Of course the ghosts are keeping me company. I'll wait till you get back before I hire an exorcist. Hope your mom gets through this ok."

Maja replies with a smiley and a heart emoji. Joel puts down his phone and looks at the ghosts.

Joel: Now buzz off.

The next day, at Joel's office, he looks tired again. He is standing at his desk when Isabella walks by.

Isabella: I thought you were getting sleep.
Joel: Maja went to take care of her mom. I still can't sleep.
Isabella: You'll get through this.

Isabella gives him a hug. Anjelica walks past the scene on the way to her cube. Isabella then leaves and goes to her cube, past Anjelica's cube. As she goes by, she looks at Anjelica who smiles but shakes her head no.

The next day, Saturday, Joel is at Battery Park, sitting on a park bench which faces the Statue of Liberty. He is nodding off. He is tired, unshaven and the people that walk by wonder if he's homeless. His phone rings. It's Maja. She is in the hospital hallway outside her mom's room.

Joel: Heyyyyyyyy.

Maja: Hiiiiiiiii.

Joel: How's your mom?

Maja: The surgery went well.

Joel: Good.

Maja: Now the recovery and the chemo start.

Joel: Hmmmmmm

Maja: Listen Joel, I could be here awhile. A long while.

Joel: Whatever you have to do. How long do you guess?

Maja: I don't know but they say her recovery will be months and her chemo could be months easy.

Joel: I understand.

Maja: It's not going to be a couple weeks.

Joel: OK.

Maja: Obviously there is something great between us but what if I'm here a year?

Joel: I don't like where this is going.

Maja: Let's be real Joel. I can call you when I get back but I think you would be better off without me.

Joel: What!

Maja: We'll meet again but I can't keep you to myself while absent for a whole year. So go date. Enjoy your life.

Joel: Maja, you are the only thing that makes me enjoy my life.

Maja: That's nice. Maybe we can pick up when I get back, but it could be a year. I'm just saying. Meet other women. Date. Have fun. It's ok.

He starts crying.

Joel: No Maja. No.

Maja: Maybe I can check in sometime. I'm not saying goodbye. I'm just saying have fun. It's ok.

Joel: No....

The doctor shows up and goes into Maja's mother's room.

Maja: The doctor just walked into my mom's room. I gotta go.

She hangs up.

CHAPTER 16

WHAT NOW

It's night. Joel can't sleep. He's on the couch. The ghosts are staring at him. He looks at Maja's window and the lights are off. He looks at his place and the ghosts are still staring.

Joel: Oh this sucks. You ghosts have got to go. The only reason you are here is because of Maja and now she's gone…and meeting who knows how many French guys. Tomorrow I'm calling an exorcist.

He roles over and turns his back to the ghosts but he knows they are still there. He turns over again and sees them all floating and starting at him. He rolls over back again. His thoughts are of Maja. Her smile, the sparkle in her eyes when she looks him, the great conversations, her laugh, her understanding of who he is. The memories are wonderful but they also hurt because she basically broke up with him. Her reasons were sound but it still stinks. He misses her.

He manages to get a few hours of sleep. The next morning, Joel stays home and calls his boss.

Will: Hello.
Joel: Hey Will, it's Joel.
Will: Hey. What's up?
Joel: Will, I'm calling in sick.
Will: All right. Sleep issues reaching extremes?
Joel: They have been at extremes for awhile. Now, on top of that, the woman I was seeing went to take care of her mom in Europe and I may never see her again. I really need a few days off. In fact, lets call it a week.
Will: Joel. I understand but believe it or not, taking a whole week will make you nuts too. All you'll do is think about her. Take a few days. If you need more, just let me know.
Joel: That makes sense. Actually, I was going to ask for an accommodation at work anyway.

Will: In what way?

Joel: My sleep issue is wiping me out. Most of my job is done on the computer. It takes me an hour to get here and then an hour to get home. That's two hours I could be working or trying to sleep.

Will: Why don't you move closer to the hospital?

Joel: What, and have my rent double? Besides, do you know how hard it is to find an apartment? Whenever an apartment issue comes up, everyone says "just move" like your just walking across the street. Listen, I'm good at my job, but my sleep problem has been going a long time and it isn't going away.

Will: Hmmmmm

Joel: Will, you've seen me. I'm a zombie.

Will: Yeah, OK. Why not.

Joel: Thanks.

Will: We have staff meetings on Wednesdays. At least be here those days.

Joel: You got it.

Will: And on Wednesdays you can take all the sales calls that come in.

Joel: OK.

Will hangs up the phone. Isabella walks by.

Will: Hey Isabella.

Isabella: Yes.

Will: Joel is going to be out a few days. Can you take the window today?

Isabella: Sure. Is he ok?

Will: Yeah, he just needs a couple days off. He just broke up with his girlfriend.

Isabella: Oh, ok.

She walks away with a smile on her face and a sparkle in her eyes.

CHAPTER 17

CHANGES

A few days later, an exorcist is dancing around Joel's apartment in very strange clothing while chanting and shaking things that make noise. Gina is there and she is loving the display.

Joel: Why did I do this?

Gina takes a picture with her phone.

At 2am that night, Joel is awake in bed.

Joel: Of course I can't sleep. The ghosts are gone though. I can't believe the exorcism worked. OK, screw this. I'm going to sell all this crap. No. Why give it away. A little money is better than nothing. First the bed.

He gets out of bed, straightens the sheets and comforter and then takes a picture of the bed. Then he backs off and takes a wider picture. Then he takes photos of the living room and all its things.

Joel: Craigslist here I come. He talks while he types on the computer: *I'm selling this bed ($400), the night stands ($20), kitchen table ($100), book case ($50) and lamps ($20 each).* Click the Next button. Yes it all looks OK. And click Publish. Boom. Why have I kept this bed anyway. It's kind of effeminate. No, it IS effeminate. I'm such a dope.

He looks through the window. Maja's lights are off.

Later, that day, in France, Maja is cleaning up around her mom's home. The nurse / friend Camille is helping her. Camille is closer to the mother's age than Maja's.

Maja: Hi mom. How did it go?
Camille: The doctor said it looks good. If it heals well, in 3 to 6 more weeks she can start chemotherapy.
Maja's Mother: What she said.

Maja sits down, takes out her phone, opens the text area for Joel. She types "Hi." But deletes it and puts her phone down.

At Joel's office, Joel is talking to his computer.

Joel: It's been a week. If I don't sell anything by the end of the day, maybe I will just give it away. C'mon computer. Bring me a customer.

The computer makes a ping noise.

Joel: Maybe I should be a computer whisperer.

       The email reads - "Hi. I am moving into

the my

       first apartment. Will you sell the bed for

$300?"

Oh geeze.

       (He types and talks a reply) How about

350?

Isabella: Hi Joel. How is everything?

Joel: I still can't sleep. I'm selling all my stuff. But the Yankees won last night.

Isabella leans in a whispers so the others don't hear what she is about to say.

Isabella: Listen, you could use a nice home cooked meal. How about you come over and we can talk and maybe you can forget about everything for an evening.

Joel stares at her and then whispers back.

Joel: I'm gonna be honest. I'm a mess. I don't want to inflict that on you and I don't know if I could handle it anyway. Thanks though.

The computer pings. The reply asks for $325.

He responds: Sure, I'll take 325 if you pick it up tonight around 7 or 8pm. I'm in the West Village. What's your number. I'll call when I get home from work.

They reply: Deal. Here's my number. 212.....

Joel: Yes!

That evening, Joel is watching the girl who wanted the bed, and her two guy friends, take the last of the bed parts out of his place. When they are gone, he closes the door and looks at the bedroom.

Joel: That feels good. Medusa's bed is gone. I'm going to celebrate by going to bed early. Well, going to couch early.

He's putting sheets on the couch and he looks out the window. Maja's lights are off. He puts the clock radio from the bedroom on the table next to the couch. It's 8:30pm. He goes to sleep but he keeps waking up.

A week later at Joel's office.

Anjelica: Hi, you only look half comatose.
Joel: Yes. I got half a night's sleep.
Anjelica: How did that happen?
Joel: I sold Medusa's bed.
Anjelica: Huh?
Joel: I mean I sold my bed. I think Maja was right; the furniture etc is causing my insomnia. So I'm getting rid of all my stuff.
Simon: I need a lamp if you've got one.

Joel: I do. I'll send you a link to the internet ad which has pictures of all the stuff in my place.

Joel sends the link to Simon.

Anjelica: So your plan is to live without anything?
Joel: No. I'll get new stuff bit by bit. I just need to get rid of all the things the ex bought.
Anjelica: How's it going with Maja?
Joel: It isn't.
Simon: Yeah. I'll take two of these lamps.
Joel: Ok. Come over after work. In fact why don't you guys all come over and we'll have a drink. I promise I won't talk about... you know who.
Tan: Sounds good. I'll be there.
Isabella: Me too.
Joel: Now if you'll excuse me, I have to work the window.

Joel goes to the sales window and opens it to see a line of salespeople.

Salesperson 12: Good morning.
Joel: Hi.

Salesperson 12: My company is introducing all new versions of their enemas and suppositories. Let me show you the details.

In France:

Maja: How's my mom?

Camille: She's sleeping. She said that was the best meal she's ever had. Where did you learn to make Shrimp Scampi?

Maja smiles.

CHAPTER 18

OTHERS

After work, Joel goes home, stops at the corner grocery and picks up things for his work mates who are on the way. He walks in to his apartment with a bag from the grocery store, puts it on the kitchen counter and starts unpacking starting with the wine and beer. He opens up the window and looks across the street. Maja's lights are off. There is a knock at the door. It's the co-workers from the office.

Joel: Hey, c'mon in.

Simon: We all took the subway together.

Anjelica: Tan is buying something at the store downstairs.

Joel: Shoes off please.

Simon: Shoes?

Joel: Yeah.

Simon and the others remove their shoes.

Simon: May I ask why?

Joel: Do you know what dogs and people do on the streets out there?

Simon: Good point.

Anjelica: I hope you don't mind; I told my husband to join us. He's on the way.

Joel: Oh great!

Isabella: The neighborhood is so charming.

Joel: Yeah. My grandparents bought this place decades ago. Otherwise I could never afford to live here.

Tan arrives.

Tan: Cool building.

Joel: Thanks.

He points at the pile of shoes and Tan removes his.

Joel: I've got beer, wine or water. Help yourself. I was going to say everything is half price but just take what you want.

Simon: I definitely want the lamps.

Isabella is looking around and touching some things like she is soaking in the aura. At one point she leans into the couch and smells it to take in Joel's odor. It turns her on.

There is a knock at the door. Joel motions to Anjelica that she can answer it since they know it's her husband. She does.

Anjelica: Hi honey.

Robert: Hi.

They kiss.

Anjelica: (To Robert) Shoes. (To everyone) Joel, everyone, this is my husband Robert.

They all say hi.

Robert: Nice to meet you all.

Joel: Have a look around.

Robert: Thanks. So you are getting rid of everything?

Joel: Everything except the TV. Actually, what the hell. That too.

Robert: Are you moving?

Everyone makes a sound like the question is a mistake.

Robert: What?

Joel: That's ok. I'm just starting over.

Robert: What's her name.

Anjelica: Robert!

Simon: Dude.

Joel: One is Maja. The other I like to refer to as Medusa.

Robert: Oh, the demon with snakes for hair. Nice. On any dating apps?

Joel: No and never will be. All those things are just data exchanges and half the data is false.

Robert: Yeah but there are some hot women on there.

Anjelica: Robert he doesn't want to talk about this.

Robert: OK. OK. Sorry.

Joel: Even if I did use the apps, guys can't win on there. When a woman puts a profile up, she gets hundreds of responses in the first few days; the men just get a few responses over hundreds of days...if they are lucky. It takes a tremendous amount of work to break through the noise. Never mind that you haven't even met them so everyone's perceptions are based on bullshit.

Isabella: I agree.

Isabella goes into that bathroom and looks around. At one point she smells the towels.

Robert: Honey, what do you think of this kitchen table?

Joel: Sorry, I hit the play button again.

People are drinking and talking and it turns out to be a nice night. After, they put their shoes on. Simon leaves with two lamps and Tan has an end table.

Simon: Thanks man.

Tan: See you at work tomorrow.

Joel: Oh, I will be working from home.

Anjelica: We'll think about the table.

Robert: And the TV. Nice to meet you.

Joel: You too.

Anjelica: Good night.

Isabella is taking towels. She comes up to him and stares in his eyes.

Isabella: Is it ok to take your towels?

Joel: Yeah sure. Take anything.

Isabella: I left you one so you don't drip everywhere.

Joel: Thanks.

Isabella: If you run out, you are welcome to come over and take a shower at my place. (She has Joel's attention). Here's my number in case of emergencies or if the mood strikes you. She puts the piece of paper in his hand and closes it. Joel is speechless. Then she kisses him gently on the cheek and leaves. The rest are in the elevator and poking their heads out to watch. They hold the elevator and it starts making a buzzing sound because the doors have been open too long. Isabella walks down the hall in a slow, sexy manner hoping Joel is watching her walk away. He is. When Isabella gets in the elevator, Anjelica smiles at her with a smirk.

It's autumn in France. The leaves are changing. At a hospital in France, Maja's mom is being take back to the treatment room.

Maja: OK mom, I will be here.

Maja sits down in the waiting room.

Nurse: Madam LaCroix?
Mrs. LaCroix: Oui.

Her son helps her and then sits down near Maja.

Luc: (in French) My mother is here for radiation. Yours too?
Camille to Maja: He said "My mother is here for radiation. Yours too?"

Maja: I don't speak French. How do you say that in French?

Luc: It's OK, I speak English.

Camille: He said he speaks English.

Maja: (To Camille) I got that. (To Luc) Chemo.

Luc: It's rough on her.

Maja: The surgery was tough.

Luc: This is the second time my mother has had cancer. It's always tough. You are American?

Maja: Yes. This is my mother's nurse, Camille.

Luc: Hello. I'm Luc.

Camille: Hi.

Maja: Hi. I'm Maja.

Luc: Where are you from?

Maja: New York.

Nurse: Luc LaCroix?

Luc: Oui.

The nurse motions to him to go to his mother. Nice to meet you both.
He leaves.

Camille: He's cute.

CHAPTER 19

THOUGHTS

Joel shows up at a cafe to meet Gina and her husband, Sean, for lunch. Gina a Sean are already seated at a table.

Joel: Ahhh, the husband. It's been too long. I haven't seen you in awhile.

They shake hands.

Sean: Yeah, I've been traveling for work a lot.
Waitress: Hi. Can I get you anything?
Joel: Just got here. Give me a minute? Thanks.
Sean: Gina said the exorcism was quite an experience.

Joel: No argument here.

Sean: Did it work?

Joel: Actually the ghosts are gone.

Sean: Really?

Gina: Really?

Joel: Yeah, but I still don't sleep well. So I've been selling or giving away everything in my apartment and it has helped a little.

Sean: I don't understand.

Gina: His ex was the one who bought all the furniture.

Sean: Oh, Medusa.

Gina laughs and beer comes out her nose.

Joel: Exactly. So someone told me all that stuff in my place is reminding me of Medusa and they suggested I should get rid of it.

Sean: Ah.

Gina: You know what I was thinking? Maybe you need to be in the company of others more. Why don't you do some volunteer work?

Joel: Huh. That's a good idea.

Sean: So, seeing anyone?

Joel gives Gina a look.

Sean: Did I hit a sore point?

Joel: Little bit.

Waitress: Would you like a drink?

Joel: Do you serve beer in any of those big steins?

Waitress: Yes we do.

Joel: Can I get an IPA in the biggest stein you have? And a mushroom burger, medium.

Waitress: Righteeo.

Joel: Thanks.

Sean: Have you tried any dating apps?

Joel throws his arms up in the air. Gina plops her head in her arms resting on the table.

Joel: Maybe I'll get a shot too.

When he gets home, we see his apartment is looking sparse as he has gotten rid of a lot of stuff. He turns off the light to go to sleep. He looks across the street and Maja's lights are off. He crawls onto the couch and gets in the fetal position.

Joel: At least the ghosts kind of kept me company.

At the hospital in France, Maja is in the waiting room alone. Her mother is in the back getting chemo. Luc walks in with his mom. They go to the window to check in and the nurse brings the mom right back. Luc sits near Maja.

Luc: Hello again.
Maja: Hi

Maja is torn. There is something attractive about this guy that she likes but she misses Joel and thinks about Joel every day. She feels unfaithful even talking to Luc.

Luc: This is my mother's last treatment. They think it's worked.
Maja: Congratulations.
Luc: Is your friend with you?

Maja: No, she stayed home this time.

Nurse: Maja?

The nurse makes a motion asking her to come back.

Maja: Gotta go.

Luc: Uh Maja. Let's have dinner some time.

Maja looks at him and doesn't know what to do.

It's Wednesday morning in New York. Joel is groggy from lack of sleep. He goes through his morning routine and leaves for work. He falls asleep on the subway and misses his stop. He wakes up and realizes what he did. At the next stop he goes across to the other platform and catches the next train back. He eventually finds his way to the hospital and his office.

Will: Yo Joel. It's window day. A little late.

Joel: Yeah, I fell asleep on the train and missed my stop.

Will: Oh man. So selling all your stuff isn't working?

Joel: It helped a bit, but …basically, I don't know. I'll get the window.

He opens the window to see salespeople.

Joel: OK. Batter up.

Salesperson 13: Hi, we just released a new type of gauze that is great for soaking up fluids like pus.

Joel: I'll be right back.

He goes to Will's office.

Will: What's up?

Joel: You know, before I started working here, I never realized how disgusting the human body is.

Will laughs. Joel goes to his desk, looks something up on the internet and makes a phone call.

Joel: Hi, do you need any volunteers?

After Work, Joel gets on the subway (the A train) to go home. He falls asleep on the train. The occasional person notices as the train goes from stop to stop. It goes past his home's stop, past Wall Street, through Brooklyn, past JFK airport and to the end of the line in Rockaway. The subway employee nudges him.

Subway Employee: Hey.

Joel keep sleeping so the employee nudges Joel again.

Subway Employee: Hey.

Joel wakes up, groggy.

Joel: What.
Subway Employee: End of the line.

Joel looks around confused.

Joel: Oh shit.

Joel gets off the train and finds his way to the return train platform. He waits awhile until it comes by. Then he hops on and heads back. As he nears the Brooklyn Bridge, he falls asleep again. This time when he wakes up, He gets off the train to find he is at the stop where he got on hours ago. He goes up to the street and hails a cab.

Joel: West Village please. Perry Street.

The next day, Maja wakes up early at her mother's place in France. Camille is already up and preparing food in the kitchen.

Maja: It's 5am. You are making breakfast?
Camille: Why not. So, what are you going to do about the cute guy?
Maja: I don't know.
Camille: You should go out with him?
Maja: I don't know.

Camille: You've been here a few months. Has Joel contacted you?

Maja: I told him not to. Actually, I told him to date other people.

Camille: Why?

Maja: I knew I would be here a long time and I figured a clean break would be easier on us.

Camille: How did he take it?

Maja: He was crying.

There is a long pause as that statement hangs in the air. Maja feels terrible.

Camille: How do you feel about it?

Maja: I think I did the right thing, but I didn't want to and it hurts.

Camille: Well, you are here in France, that French guy is cute, it's just dinner. Why not?

Maja's Mother: Camille?

Camille goes in the other room. Maya picks up her phone. She opens the text area for Joel and thinks. At that very moment, Joel is laying on the couch and looking at the text that Maja last sent months ago.

Joel: The miserable have no other medicine, but only hope.

He puts the phone down on the floor and stares at the ceiling. Just then the three dots start moving on his phone because Maja is typing a text to Joel. "I've been thinking of you." But she pauses and then erases the text. The dots go away. She puts the phone down and walks into another room. Joel rolls over, picks the phone up off the floor and starts to type a text to her "I miss you." But he remembers her breaking up with him. He deletes his text.

Joel: I'm never going to see her again. Damnit.

He gets up and paces back and forth in his apartment for a five minutes.

Joel: Nothing. Nothing!

He has a tantrum, jumping and kicking and yelling and spazzing out.

Joel: I can't go on like this. It's been months. Months! The last time we spoke she told me to date other people… and then she hung up on me. I don't want to date other people. I can't call her; she hung up on me. She hasn't even reached out to say hi. Nothing! I can't get closure. I don't want closure. I will never see her again. This is driving me crazy.

He lies down on the floor and stares up at the ceiling. Then picks up his phone and calls someone.

Joel: Hi. I hope it's not too late.
Isabella: No, it's fine.

CHAPTER 20

A FRIENDLY VISIT

Later that night, there is a knock on the door. Joel opens it.

Isabella: Hi.
Joel: Hi.

Isabella walks in, takes off her shoes and puts her purse on the kitchen counter. She is wearing a brown leather jacket, jeans, a white t-shirt.

Joel: Wow, you look amazing.
Isabella: Thank you.
Joel: Especially considering that I woke you up.
Isabella: I'm glad you did. You look nice too.

She takes off her jacket and puts it on the counter. She is not wearing a bra. She moves in close. She looks really irresistible. She puts her hands on his chest. They look deeply at each other. Then both of her hands slowly grab onto his shirt and she pulls him in. They kiss. Her lips are like honey. She is filled with desire as she has fantasized about him for so long. As she kisses him, she moans.

She breathes heavy as their lips part. She reaches down and unbuttons his jeans. Then he takes off her shirt and she unbuttons her jeans. They embrace again with passionate kisses. They are thinking the same thing - clothing sucks. They break and like it's a race, quickly remove what clothing they still have on. Before you know it, they are naked and he is on top of her on the couch. Her legs are wrapped around him as they screw. It is very intense.

Afterwards, she is under sheets on the couch and he brings over a blanket and cuddles up with her.

Joel: Listen, no offense, but we work together and I really don't want anyone at work knowing about this.

Isabella: Same here.

Joel: Good.

Isabella: But to be honest, I think they might be picking up on something.

Joel: Yeah well, let them make assumptions.

Isabella: Yes.

Joel: If we tell them, we will never hear the end of it.

Isabella: True.

She snuggles in.

Isabella: This is a comfortable couch.

Joel: Yeah.

Twenty minutes later…

Isabella: Are you asleep?

Joel: Never.

Isabella: Good.

She roles over, kisses him and they have sex again. This time she is on top most of the way. Joel has always noticed her beauty but never imagined she would be naked and having sex with him on his couch. She's so hot, he feels like he is in a movie. Every time he sees her, she looks beautiful. But now this gorgeous sexy woman with the hottest body he has ever seen, is stark naked, riding him and letting loose. And as she's going, sometimes she makes a low pitched moan and sometimes its a breathy grunt. Her animal side combined with her beauty is amazing. As she orgasms she lets out a high pitched squeal. She is thankful that he held on for her. She kisses him, takes his hands, puts them on her breasts and keeps riding him. A few minutes later she has a second orgasm and it coincides with his.

30 minutes afterwards, as they are cuddling on the couch again, Isabella has a question.

Isabella: I'm a little dehydrated. Got any water?
Joel: Yeah.

They walk to the kitchen sink naked. Joel gets glasses, fills them up with water and they both take a drink.

Joel: Not to put a damper on things, but even outside of work, I'm still kind of a mess and not sure I want this to go anywhere. I don't know what I want.

Isabella: That's OK. I'm glad we connected.

Joel: Geeze, you are so beautiful.

Isabella: Thanks.

She takes another drink of water. While she is drinking, he says:

Joel: Some people don't look good naked. But you even look sexy drinking water.

She puts the glass on the counter.

Isabella: You know, we've been going at it a while and I'm feeling a little dirty.

Joel: You mean you want to go home?

Isabella: I mean I think I need a shower. Want to take a shower?

The next thing you know they are in the shower having sex. She is up against the shower wall with her legs around him as they fuck.

Afterwards, She dries herself off with the only towel he has left. Then she remembers she took the others.

Isabella: Oh, I forgot, this is your only towel.
Joel: That's ok. I have plenty of paper towels.

They go into the kitchen and Joel uses a lot of paper towels drying himself off. Then they head to the couch again. They get under the covers. Joel is spooning Isabella on the couch and he thinks to himself *"Now, I should be able to sleep tonight."* He looks at the clock and it's 2 am. Isabella fell right to sleep. At 3 am he is still awake. He looks tired. Some time after that he drifts off to sleep.

The alarm clock wakes them up at 6am. Isabella wakes up and doesn't feel Joel next to her which is odd since its a couch not a spacious bed. She finds the clock radio and looks at the buttons until she figures out how to turn it off. Then she looks down and sees he is curled up on the floor on an exercise mat.

Isabella: Joel?
Joel: Yeah.
Isabella: You didn't sleep, did you.
Joel: Not really.
Isabella: You poor baby. Anything I can do?
Joel: Uh.

Isabella crawls off the couch. She starts caressing him all over. Joel was glad they had all the sex that they did last night. However he got it out of his system and he didn't want this new relationship to encompass his life. He wanted his relationship with Maja to encompass his life, but that was over. On the other hand he truly likes Isabella and she is quite a breathtaking woman. And she's touching him. But he's exhausted.

Joel: Uh, Isabella.
Isabella: Yes?
Joel: Isabella, I just can't. I'm soooo tired.
Isabella: Oh.

Joel: I'm glad you are here though.

They cuddle for a minute.

Isabella: Hey Joel?

Joel: Yeah?

Isabella: I'm just curious. It's Saturday.

Joel: Yeah?

Isabella: Why did the alarm go off?

Joel: It's Saturday? It's Saturday. Oh. Oh, shit. I have to go. I'm volunteering.

Isabella: OK.

Joel: I don't mean to rush you out, but I made a commitment.

Isabella: It's ok.

He kisses her. Then they get up and get dressed.

Isabella: What kind of volunteer work?

Joel: Well, a few things.

He stops talking as he is watching this beautiful woman put on her clothes. She pulls up the thing she wore and puts on her t-shirt. She looks over at him staring at her. She walks over and kisses him.

Isabella: Want to go again?
Joel: Um. Yeah.

She takes off her t-shirt.

Joel: Wait. I can't.

She moves in and kisses his neck.

Joel: Volunteer…Commitment…Can't.
Isabella: OK.

She puts her t-shirt on. He is staring at her and weakening. She takes off her t-shirt again and puts her arms around him and starts up again.

Joel: Uh. Volunteer. Commitment.

They are kissing. He is lost in his head. Then he snaps out of it.

Joel: No. I have to help people. They are relying on me to be there.

Isabella: Ok.

He gives her a quick peck. She puts her t-shirt back on.

Isabella: So you were going to tell me what you are doing today.

Joel: Right. This morning I'm helping at a homeless shelter. This afternoon at an animal rescue and tomorrow I'm learning neighborhood disaster training from FEMA.

Isabella: That's a lot.

Joel: Yeah. Someone suggested it to keep mind mind off of....you know.

Isabella: Good idea.

Joel: Yeah, but I may be overdoing it.

Isabella: Well, we can stay here if you like.

Joel: I mean over committing my time. Plus I'm thinking of doing more.

Isabella looks concerned. They get dressed and walk out the door. Joel watches her walk down the hall to the elevator again. She knows he's watching. She walks back and takes his hand.

Isabella: C'mon.

She walks him to the elevator and they go down stairs. Then they walk outside.

Joel: I'm going this way.
Isabella: I'm going the other.
Joel: Glad you came over.
Isabella: Me too. Call me tonight, if you want. (She kisses him).
Joel: Bye.

He watches her walk away for a few seconds and then walks off in his direction.

CHAPTER 21

VOLUNTEERING

Joel goes to a homeless shelter to serve food. There are many people in shabby clothes and who clearly haven't taken a shower in a long time. He feels sorry for them and is glad he can help in some way. He also feels grateful for all he has, especially considering what he experienced last night. After serving food, he helps clean up and then helps prepare for later meals.

From there he goes to an animal shelter. He helps feed the animals and he cleans out their cages.

Animal Shelter Employee: We need to wash all the new animals we bring in. Just in case they have something that might infect the other animals.

Joel: OK.

They walk over to the washing room. And she shows Joel the procedure.

Animal Shelter Employee: We have a big table and basin for the animals here. It has a mat so they don't get their feet stuck in the drain. There is a sprayer for the water, soap here and towels there. Most of them are afraid but once you soap them up, they seem to be ok when they know you aren't going to hurt them. Just talk to them nicely and it will be ok.

Joel washes a few new dogs who were brought in after someone inspects them for disease or injuries. He likes one little dog. He picks it up when he is drying it off.

Joel: Oh you are so cute.

It licks his face.

The next day, Sunday, he goes to the FEMA office to train for disaster management.

FEMA Trainer: Welcome everyone to training for disasters that affect neighborhoods. For those who don't necessarily know, FEMA stands for Federal Emergency Management Agency. It is an agency set up under President Jimmy Carter in 1978. The agency's primary purpose is to coordinate the response to a disaster that has occurred in the United States and that overwhelms the resources of local and state authorities.

This training is called CERT which stands for Community Emergency Response Team. It covers basic skills that are important to know in a disaster when emergency services are not available, so people in the neighborhood can know what to do. Lets open our workbooks to page 1.

CHAPTER 22

THE DATE

In the evening a few days later, Maja shows up at a restaurant in France and Luc is in a waiting area. She is dressed in a hot black dress.

Luc: Hello Maja. You look great.
Maja: Thanks.

Luc kisses her on both cheeks. She is not used to it. They go to the hostess stand.

Luc: (In French) Table for two?
Hostess: (In French) It will be about 30 minutes. May I get your name?
Luc: Luc.

Hostess: (In French) Have a seat at the bar.

They go to the bar.

Luc: Does Red wine sound good?

Maja: Yes.

Luc: (In French) Two Merlots please. (To Maja) How is your mother?

Maja: She's been better. She has one more chemo treatment to go. It's making her sick.

Luc: Yes, my mother had the same problem.

Maja: I'm very worried.

The bartender brings them their wine.

Luc: Cheers.

Maja: Cheers.

Maja hesitates hearing those words. She just said she is worried. Suddenly she feels not only like a hypocrite, but also that she isn't being honest even with herself. She told Joel to date others and then cut ties with him. Even though it was logical, she hates herself for doing this and hates that she's on a date.

Maja: Luc, I can't do this. I can't be cheery. I'm worried about my mom. I'm only in France temporarily. And I was seeing a guy before I left who I really like and I keep thinking about him. And like an idiot, I told him to date other people and I'm hating myself for doing it. But bottom line, I can't do this, and I'm sorry.

She runs out of the restaurant. She takes cab home looking out the window the whole time and thinking of Joel.

CHAPTER 23

BREAK THE SILENCE

When Maja gets to her mom's place, she sits on the front steps and texts Joel.

MAYA'S TEXT

Joel, I think of you often and hope you are well. My mother is still taking chemo. I don't know how much longer I will be here. But I'm so sorry I hurt you. I miss you. Call me if you don't hate me or even if you do but would like to talk to me.

She presses send and wonders if she will hear from Joel. Ten seconds later her phone rings.

Joel: Hi.

Maja: (Starts crying). Hi.

Joel: Why are you crying?

Maja: I'm just happy to talk to you.

Joel: I'm glad you reached out. I thought about you a lot. If it helps, I was crawling the walls missing you but I felt like you didn't want me to call you.

Maja: I didn't know how to handle all this.

Joel: Yeah, moving away for an indefinite time, there's no right answer. (Pause) It's so nice to hear your voice. I've missed you.

Maja: Same here.

Joel: So I took your advice and got rid of most of my stuff.

Maja: Really!

Joel: Yeah, I have been selling it but it's surprisingly difficult to sell used furniture.

His couch is now gone. He just has an air mattress and a few things.

Maja: Are the ghosts still there?

Joel: (laughs) No. They left after I hired an exorcist. You should have seen that.

Maja: Wish I had. How's the sleep.

Joel: A little better but not great. When I sold the bed, my sleep improved. But it has never been solid. I think you are what made the difference.

Maja: I love you.

Joel: I love you too.

There is a long pause as they both feel happy they each said that.

Joel: How's your mom?

Maja: Up and down. She has one more treatment to go but it's making her sick. She's losing weight and vomiting.

Joel: That's terrible. I'm sorry. Maybe talk to the doctor and see if they should stop. It's worth asking and talking it out.

Maja: OK. It couldn't hurt to ask. Thanks.

Joel: So... I started doing volunteer work.

Maja: Really. What brought that on.

Joel: To be honest, you. I keep looking across the street and see your lights are off and I needed something to occupy my thoughts more.

Maja: Awwwwww.

Joel: There is a really cute dog at the animal shelter. If no one adopts him soon, I will.

Maja: That's great. So, I don't want to poke the bear, but have you seen anyone?

Joel: No Maja.

Maja: Oh good.

Joel: No Maja, I mean you don't get to ask that and I will never answer it because...no answer will ever be the right answer. If I say I did, you will hate me for what <u>you</u> caused. If I say I didn't, you will never be 100% sure that I'm telling you the truth and it will hang over us forever. The fact of the matter is you opened Pandora's box and the evil can not be put back.

You will just have to accept that. You can't look back. It won't help in any way.

Maja: Shit. You are right.

Joel: So tell me about your mom. Not her sickness. I mean about her.

Maja: Well, she is originally from France. She and my dad met when...

They talk for hours until literally the sun comes up.

Maja: Oh, how pretty. The Sun is rising.

Joel: The Sun is rising? Oh no.

Maja: What's the problem?

Joel: We've been talking for hours. I called France and I don't have an international calling plan. This call is going to cost me a thousand dollars!

Maja: Oh no! (she laughs)

Joel: I guess I'll be sleeping on the floor for awhile.

Maja: Call the phone company. Maybe you can find a sympathetic person who can apply a plan starting yesterday.

Joel: Oh, I hope so or I'll be stealing food from the cafeteria for a year.

Maja: So glad you called though.

Joel: Me too.

They hang up. Joel goes to sleep and sleeps through the night.

CHAPTER 24

SPENDING TIME

It's Wednesday morning at Joel's office. They are in the morning meeting.

Anjelica: Say Joel, you look rested.
Joel: Well, I'm averaging 5 hours of sleep per night.
Will: That's better at least.
Tan: How did that happen?
Isabella: Sell all your stuff?
Joel: Most of it. I'm also working through things.

He doesn't want to bring up Maja and upset Isabella. Especially in the meeting in front of her co-workers.

Will: Ready to work the window?

Joel: I look forward to hearing about the latest vomit bags and adult diapers.

The meeting breaks. Joel puts his stuff at his desk and heads to the sales window. He is about to open it when his phone beeps. It's a text from Isabella.

Isabella text: Like to meet after work?
Joel text: I have to take a FEMA class but maybe for a bit?
Isabella text: OK.
Joel text: A few blocks away is a corner of Central Park. How about we meet there at Columbus Circle?
Isabella text: Sounds fun.

At the end of the day, everyone has left. Joel exits the hospital and walks over to meet Isabella at the park. She has never looked better. She unbuttoned an extra button to show off her cleavage. She smiles as he approaches.

Isabella: Hi.

Joel: Hi Isabella.

She hugs him and he can't help but hug her back.

Isabella: What did you have in mind?

Joel: I'm sorry Isabella but I cannot continue this.

Isabella: What's wrong?

Joel: It's not you. I reconnected with my girlfriend. I just can't see anyone else. That night we spent together was really great but the thought of being involved with anyone else in any intimate way just makes me feel like I'm betraying her and it makes me feel sad. I'm sorry.

Isabella: So this is why you wanted to meet?

Joel: I like you and didn't want to blow you off or play those horrible games people play with each other by trying to avoid a difficult conversation or gain power over someone. You deserve respect and honesty.

Isabella: Thank you. So she is back from Europe?

Joel: Not yet.

Isabella: Uh…

Joel: I just can't do it. Isabella, you are nice and have a good heart and when our office goes out to lunch, I see guys all the time noticing you. You are a stunningly beautiful woman. I can't even believe you are interested in me.

Isabella: Well, I am. Good guys are hard to find. So listen, go do your volunteer thing. And feel free to call me if you ever just want to fuck.

She leaves.

Joel: That thought's not going to help my sleep.

At night, Joel is lying on his couch wide awake.

Joel: Damnit.

Month's later, it's Thanksgiving. At the Homeless Shelter, there are a lot of people who showed up to volunteer for Thanksgiving meals. The Director addresses them all.

Homeless Shelter Director: Hello everybody. Happy Thanksgiving.
Everyone: Happy Thanksgiving.

Homeless Shelter Director: I'm glad you all came by. We will break you up into groups for different chores like carving turkey or working the food line or wrapping utensils in napkins, etc. But before we get started, just like you all and myself, the people we are helping today, like to eat every day. It would be really great if you could find it in your hearts to also volunteer on other days throughout the year. Even seldomly. Every little bit counts. Now Joel here will organize who does what. Once again, I'm glad you all came by and enjoy your holiday.

Joel: OK. Who here can I trust with a knife to carve the turkeys?

Many volunteers are doing chores and many homeless people are coming in and eating.

Wednesday at the hospital. Joel is at the window.

Salesperson 14: We sell pouches and bags for urinary care.

Salesperson 15: Oh, that's what we sell too.

At FEMA training:

FEMA Trainer: ...That takes care of flooding. Next up, power blackouts. If you will turn to page 121 of your workbooks.

At the animal shelter, Joel is putting out food for all the dogs. He is petting them too.

Joel: Here you go.

They are all happy.

Joel's apartment at night. He looks across the street and Maja's lights are off. There is lots of snow. His phone beeps from a text.

Maja's text: My mom's cancer is gone and she's getting better. I may be home in a week or two.
Joel responds back: GREAT!!!!!!!!!!!!!!!!!!!

That weekend, in the FEMA meeting room:
FEMA Trainer: Congratulations, you are all now certified to handle disasters in the neighborhoods.
Everyone: Yea…

Joel is volunteering at a Cat Rescue organization. He is sitting on the couch in a room with 50 cats. He doesn't look happy.

Joel: Maybe this one isn't for me.

Joel is volunteering at an elderly organization. He is wearing rubber gloves and carrying a plunger as he walks up to his supervisor.

Joel: OK, that's all 5 bathrooms. Anything else?
Supervisor: Did you get the other 5 on the 2nd floor?

Joel walks off and mumbles to himself.

Joel: Maybe I am overdoing it.
Supervisor: Huh?
Joel: Nothing

CHAPTER 25

MAJA RETURNS

A cab pulls up to Maja's building. Maja gets out, the driver gets out and get's Maja's suitcases from the trunk. She tips him and goes in the building.

In Joel's apartment, Joel feeds his new dog. His apartment is basically empty. He walks over to get the TV remote from the only end stand left and he sees Maja's lights are off. He sits down on his air mattress.

Maja enters her place. It's been a long time. Seasons ago. She takes off her shoes and leaves the suitcases at the door. She goes to the kitchen counter and sees the now dead flowers that Joel gave her many months ago. She looks out her window and sees his lights on. She texts him.

Maja's text: I'm back.

Joel gets the text and runs to the window. She waves at him. He opens his window. She opens her window.

Maja: It's freezing cold.
Joel: Want to come over and see my place and how I redecorated it?
Maja: Be right there.

They both close their windows and she goes across the street being careful not to slip in the ice and snow. She presses the buzzer for his apartment, he buzzes her in and she goes up the stairs and knocks on the door. He opens it and they have a long hug. Then she comes in. She looks around.

Maja: Wow!
Joel: It's quite the palace, huh?
Maja: Yes it is.

She sees the dog.

Maja: And who is this?
Joel: His name is Brutus.

She squats down to greet the dog.

Maja: Hi Brutus.

Brutus comes over wagging his tail and she pets him. She stands up and looks at Joel. They share a kiss and hug again.

Maja: Would you two like to come over where there is furniture?
Joel: Hmmmmm.
Maja: We can order pizza and salads.
Joel: Sounds perfect. C'mon Brutus.

Joel puts a leash on Brutus. They all walk across the street in the snow and ice. They enter Maja's apartment and Joel sees the vase with the dead flowers. She takes his hand.

Maja: What do you want on your pizza?

As the story closes, a half eaten pizza is on the coffee table, Brutus is sleeping under the coffee table and Joel and Maja, fully clothed, are sleeping on the couch in each other's arms.

THE END

About the Author

Jon Marcus is a Hollywood screenwriter who focuses on thoughtful comedies.

He went to The Ohio State University and got a BS in marketing after studying years of science classes and tutoring math. He does not have a degree in literature. He does not have an advanced degree. He did not go to an Ivy League school. He learned to write by watching a plethora of movies in an attempt to avoid his parents. He loves a good story and attributes his fondness of fiction and his sense of humor to a slightly warped mind molded by said parents. Not that he's complaining.

He is an enthusiast of science and history. He is also a romantic, not only of the way he sees the fairer sex but also in his vision of life. He has written numerous movie scripts, realized that people in Hollywood don't like to read, and he loves writing and creating thoughtful stories and fun characters. He also has a penchant for run-on sentences which he is working on and often tries to cure with commas and semicolons.

He grew up in New Jersey and eventually found his way to the West Coast. Currently, when he's not sitting alone in his dark Santa Monica home worrying about his weight, he can be found watching Pacific waves and playful dolphins from the Malibu coast and wondering what psychotic thoughts are going through the minds of seemingly normal looking people around him.